THE *Lighthouse*

Chicago's Best

Charli, Happy Reading! Katharine H.

By Katharine E. Hamilton

ISBN- 10: 10: 0-692-84906-8
ISBN-13: 978-0-692-84906-4

Chicago's Best

www.katharinehamilton.com

Cover Design by Kerry Prater.

To my Readers
Because you guys are beyond
awesome.

Acknowledgments

Many thanks to my husband, my family, and my friends for all their support. I love to write, and you all let me do that while supplying me with constant encouragement.

Thanks to my alpha and beta readers for feedback that helps shape the story.

Thanks to my editor, Lauren Hanson, for taking my rough work and turning it into something readable.

And thanks to my readers. You guys are awesome. AS ALWAYS.

« CHAPTER ONE »

THE WIND WAS A NICE reprieve from the heat as the young woman stepped into the familiar alleyway between her café and the flower shop next door. Kat Riesling wiped the back of her hand across a damp brow as she sat the heavy trash bag beside her feet and reached behind her to close the door.

"Gato!" She called in a sing song voice. "Chat! Kissa!" As she lightly tapped the sides of a metal pail, three young cats emerged from beneath the dumpster, meowing and arching eagerly against her legs in anticipation for what she carried. "How are my sweet boys today?" Kat cooed, as she rubbed generously down the soft backs and up the tails of the furry creatures. Her gaze shifted to several loose cigarette butts littering the concrete near her back door and tisked disapprovingly with her tongue. "Someone has been smoking in our alleyway again." She opened the back door to the café and reached inside for a broom, while her free hand still held the pail of scraps for the cats. "You boys be patient. I need to clean your plate." She made quick work of sweeping the butts to the side and then dumped the small samples of scraps on the ground for the cats. She then swept the butts into a dustpan and walked over to the dumpster. Raising the lid, she tossed them inside. She then walked back over to the door and grabbed the full trash bag and escorted it to the dumpster as well. As she tossed the heavy bag over the side into the tall metal container, a faint sound of discomfort filtered through the metal siding. She froze, eyes wide in surprise. Tentatively, she grabbed the lid flap and lifted it, tossing it back quickly. She then armed herself with her broomstick as she leaned over the top. Before she could scream, a firm hand shot out and covered her mouth, another hand circling her neck, creating a firm hold. A man slowly emerged from the canister, his eyes sharp and green. *A fierce green*, she thought, as he made hushing noises in a whisper.

"I need you to be quiet, okay? I am not here to harm you." He nodded towards her as if trying to trigger some sort of response from her. Her hands still gripped her broom, and her eyes shot towards it.

"Please do not hit me. I promise I will not hurt you. I am going to remove my hand now. Are you going to scream?"

She shook her head and he slowly eased his hand away. She took two full steps back from the dumpster and he admired her calm despite her fear.

"What are you doing in my dumpster?" Her words were quick, breathless, but forceful as she continued to grip the broomstick in baseball bat formation.

"I assure you, miss, that I am here under good intentions. I'm a police officer. I must ask that you go back inside and not return until another officer notifies you."

A look of disbelief washed over her face followed by annoyance. The sassy tilt to her head and the fist on her hip told him she was not going anywhere. "Right." Disbelief rang in her voice. "So I am just to believe that a strange man who litters my back stoop with cigarettes and is hiding in my dumpster is a police officer? What are you doing in the trash, Oscar the Grouch?"

His eyes shot upward in impatience. "Don't believe me, do you?" He matched her annoyance. "Look to the rooftop across the street, far East corner."

She turned and did as he said, noting an officer standing on the rooftop at the ready with a rifle of some sort. She gasped. "What the-"

"See. You are currently intruding on a potential bust. Now please go back inside and inform the rest of the employees not to venture out here until we notify you."

"How long have you guys been here?" She asked.

He sighed in frustration. "Ma'am, please. You are compromising our set up." He ducked low in the dumpster, his voice quiet. She saw a hand rise over the edge and point. "Do you mind?" He motioned towards the lid. Growling in frustration, she stood on her tiptoes to reach the black lid and began folding it back over. "You better not harm my cats," she grumbled, as she let the lid slap closed and quickly made her way back inside.

∞

Her cats? Of all the things for the woman to worry about, she was worried about three stray cats. He shook his head in dismay but could not help the small smile that spread over his face. Had the woman not been tampering down a temper, he thought she might hold quite a smile in her pretty features. The dark eyes shadowed by perfectly arched eyebrows, set within slashing cheekbones, full lips, and creamy skin, the woman was definitely beautiful. Ian O'Dell shook his head as he continued his stake out. Not the most luxurious of accommodations, but it was his turn for the dirty work. His partner, Travis Starr, had pulled back-to-back all-nighters the prior week in order to keep surveillance on this particular spot. Ian owed him. And he knew it. The thought of what lay beneath his feet grossed him out, but he tried to concentrate on the positives. They were closing in on one of the most notorious drug runners this side of the city. Drugs had yet to really venture east, but several drop points had begun to surface. Travis' girlfriend owned the small flower shop that shared the alleyway with the café, and she reported strange men lurking about a mere week ago. After Travis' incognito quest, it was confirmed that the two men seen were none other than the measly, bottom-of-the-food-chain runners for the infamous Biggs, the biggest drug boss in Chicago. This particular area of the city had yet to experience the harsh realities of the drug trade or the impact on its streets, and under Ian's watchful eyes, it was not about to start now.

He shifted, his elbow lightly bumping against the wall of the dumpster. He heard one of the cats jump on top of the roof and let out a low meow of acknowledgment. He glanced at his watch. What felt like hours, had only been twenty minutes since the cute café owner's interruption. He tried to resituate his legs, his left calf trembling as he moved, slowly cramping from being stuck in the same position for a couple of hours. He heard the sound of footsteps and froze. It was past dark, surely those were the feet of the two men and not the café worker. Hopefully his warning had been serious enough she would heed his words. He waited patiently for his signal. He would only emerge once his fellow officers cornered the men in the alley.

"Don't move!" The words muffled behind the walls of the dumpster. Ian waited a breath.

"Hands above your heads. Kneel!" A long pause, footsteps. "We said don't move!" Travis barked. A tap resounded on the dumpster and he threw back the lid just as one of the men began to run. He leapt over the side and tackled him just as he passed by, and felt the burn and crunch of his knees against the concrete beneath him. The man threw an elbow, landing it against his jaw, but Ian held strong, wrenching the man's arm behind his back, followed by the second and handcuffing him. "Nice try," he growled, as he hefted the man to his feet. He nudged him towards a fellow officer and turned to see Travis walking towards him with a wide smile. "We did it, O'Dell. Nicely done." He punched Ian on the shoulder and then grimaced. "Yikes, is that you?"

"Probably." Ian lifted his sleeve and sniffed, the dreadful scent of rotting organic matter wafting over him. "Whoa."

"Yeah." Travis interjected on a laugh. "You reek."

"Not all of us can snatch the glamorous stake out jobs, Starr."

"Glamorous? You call staying up 48 hours glamorous?" Travis acted offended.

"Compared to three hours in a city dumpster? Yeah, I do." Ian jested and shook his head as Travis slapped him on the back.

"I'll buy you a meal and a beer in compensation, how's that sound?" He gestured towards the café. "Kat normally doesn't close up the kitchen until eight."

"It's 9:30." Ian pointed out.

"Ah, but Kat owes me." Travis motioned towards the sidewalk and they walked towards the front entrance.

"Detective Starr," one of the officers walked towards them. "We'll take them down to County, but the chief wants a report by tomorrow morning."

"Tell him he'll get it. First, I owe O'Dell a meal."

"Yes sir." The officer slid into the police cruiser and pulled away from the curb.

∞

Travis opened the door to the friendly café, the smell of fresh bread making Ian's stomach grumble despite his last few hours surrounded by deteriorating scraps.

A man in his late twenties manned the order counter and looked up with an easy smile as Travis stepped forward.

"Travis, my man, what's up?" He reached across the countertop and shook Travis' hand.

"Hey Jeremiah. I was hoping I could squeeze a couple meals out of you guys tonight. We just finished a bust and we are starving."

"Oh, was that what that was?" Jeremiah motioned behind him, to the closed doors from that Ian assumed led to the kitchen and the back door to the café.

"Yep. Turns out the alleyway has been a hotspot for some lowlifes recently. We caught them though, so no worries there."

"That's good to know. Kat will be pleased. She knew someone was lurking about due to all the cigarette butts being left behind. She was not pleased with that."

Travis laughed. "I imagine not. Think you could sweet talk her for us?"

"Yeah, give me a minute." He motioned towards a table and Travis led the way to a seat.

Ian did little to hide his appraisal of the place, the high ceilings, the floor to ceiling windows that surrounded the three sides not facing the alley, the brick walls. The vintage bank building had been fully converted into a bright and welcoming space that held a modern twist to vintage surroundings.

"Starr," A familiar voice drifted over to their table and had Ian turning to find the beautiful spitfire of a woman from earlier walking towards them. "You barge in here demanding a meal?" She stood next to their table with her hands on her hips, a damp hand towel thrown over her shoulder. Her creamy brown eyes focused upon Ian. "Tired of dumpster diving?"

Travis laughed. "I guess you two have met?"

"Yes. I caught him scaring Gato, Chat, and Kissa by hiding in the trash. You smell," she stated, her eyes holding a glint of amusement.

"So I've heard," Ian mumbled, only slightly embarrassed, as he accepted the cold beer Jeremiah walked over and slid in front of him.

"So, am I free to walk about my alleyway? Did you save me from the bad guys?"

"Mock all you wish, but the situation was a serious one." The edge in Ian's voice did not go unnoticed.

"And I listened, did I not?" Kat challenged.

"It would seem so." He looked up at her and she held his gaze firmly until the corners of her lips began to lift and she began laughing. She covered her mouth with the back of her hand before reaching down and snatching a piece of greenery from his hair. A leaf, no doubt from a flower stem from the floral store next door. She cleared her throat. "I apologize. You just... wow, you really smell terrible." She laid a gentle hand on his shoulder. "I guess for saving my café from ruffians you guys deserve a hot meal. What can I get you?"

"I want my usual." Travis took a sip of his drink.

"And you, Oscar, what would you like?"

"Oscar?" Travis asked in confusion.

"Oscar the Grouch." Kat clarified, nodding towards Ian.

Travis burst into laughter. "Nice." He fist-bumped Kat.

"Hilarious." Ian replied, sarcasm dripping from his voice as he studied the menu, attempting to ignore the sexy smirk Kat flashed his way. "I'll have the club sandwich, please. And my name is Ian. Ian O'Dell." He held onto the menu as she attempted to retrieve it, making sure she looked him in the eye. She smiled as he released the menu and she tucked it under her arm.

"I'll get these out to you two in a jiff." She turned to walk away.

"And you?" Ian called after her. "A name?"

She glanced over her shoulder. "Kat Riesling. Like the wine." She winked and headed towards the kitchen.

∞

Kat placed the finishing touches on the men's orders and handed them off to Jeremiah. She then tidied up the kitchen once more and hung her apron on a hook by the door. She was done for the day, and Jeremiah would continue serving coffee and the remaining pastries until closing at midnight. She sighed as she gathered her oversized purse and placed her fedora on her head. Stepping back into the dining area, Travis waved her over.

"You talk with Sara yet?"

"No. Why?" She asked, sliding into the booth next to him and stealing one of his potato chips. As she crunched she watched his fellow officer devour his club sandwich. *He was a handsome sort*, she realized. Bright green eyes in a lean tan face, the crown of shaggy gold hair gave him the appearance of a man used to sun and sea versus the lifestyle of windy Chicago. She wondered what his story was. As her mind wandered, she felt a small jab in her side from Travis, a knowing grin on his face as he took a bite of his own sandwich.

"What were you saying?" She asked, blinking away her thoughts.

"I asked if you had talked to Sara, because she was a bit freaked out about earlier."

"No, I haven't and I am not looking forward to that conversation. Sara is such a girl."

Ian looked up at that comment in amusement and found Travis' glare. "You realize you're a girl as well, right?" Travis asked, annoyed.

"Yes, but come on, I mean seriously. You have to admit Sara overreacts to well, everything."

Travis straightened in his seat. "I would think drug runners in your alleyway would be serious enough to react to, Kat. Cut her some slack."

Kat rolled her eyes in forfeit. "Fine. By the way, thanks for the heads up." She turned to him in disappointment. "Not one officer came in here to tell me there was a drug bust going on behind my café."

"Really?" Travis scratched the scruff along his jaw. "I thought I did."

"No. So I had the pleasure of finding out by discovering Oscar here in the trash."

"Ian." Ian corrected, without glancing up.

"Sorry about that. I really thought I had told you." Travis' brow furrowed. "That could have put you at risk, Kat. I truly am sorry."

She kissed his cheek. "You're forgiven." She slid out of the booth. "I'm headed home. Be sure to leave your scraps with Jeremiah so he can feed Gato, Chat, and Kissa."

"I will." Travis grinned.

"It was interesting meeting you... Ian." Kat stated, finally receiving a look from those meadow green eyes. His mouth was full and she noted a small blush to his cheeks as he realized he could not respond. He gave a small nod in acknowledgment as she walked off. When he finally swallowed, he looked to find Travis studying him. "What?"

Travis chuckled. "I can tell you're intrigued by her."

"How's that?"

"I can just tell. I don't blame you though. She's a neat woman."

"How long have you known her?"

Travis shrugged his shoulders. "I don't know, about three years. I date Sara, the floral shop owner next door. She's Kat's best friend and also her roommate, so I come in contact with her often. In fact, I am helping them remodel their house. I'll be going over there tomorrow. Since I will wrap up the reports tonight, we don't have to show up at the station tomorrow. Care to join me for some painting? I know they'd appreciate it, as will I."

Ian pondered the idea and sipped the last of his beer. "Sure. What time?"

"Plan to head over there about nine or so."

"I could do nine. Where does she live?"

"Across the street from me." Travis stated with a smile.

Ian's brows rose. "Really? That must be convenient, living across the street from your girlfriend."

"It is." Travis winked. "Though I may have to sell the place soon if I don't find a roommate myself. The payments are killing me right now, but I don't want to rent somewhere else for the same reason."

"You need a roommate?"

"Yeah, interested?"

"You kidding?"

"No. I'm being serious. I could really use one if you are interested."

"We work together." Ian pointed out.

"Even more convenient." Travis clapped his hands as if the matter were decided. "We could dig a little deeper into some of our cases without eavesdroppers up at the precinct."

Ian leaned back in the booth as Jeremiah walked up to clear their plates. As he reached for them, Ian glanced up, "Um, Kat said something about the scraps."

Jeremiah rolled his eyes. "Yeah, I got it. She always feeds the strays. I'll take care of it." Nodding, he sped away onto the next table.

"Think about it, Ian. You would be able to move out of that nasty apartment downtown and actually have a house to live in, and in a decent neighborhood... pretty neighbors..."

Ian smirked. "Alright. I'll give it a go. However, I do not care too much for the pretty neighbors. I am more interested in a clean house to live in versus my horrible apartment complex."

"Right," Travis' disbelief evident in his response. "Well, whatever reason gets me a roommate. Let's go." Travis stood.

"Do we pay up at the counter?"

"We don't pay." Travis pulled his car keys out of his pocket. "Perks of being friends with the owner."

"Well you are her friend. I should pay."

"We'll just add it to my tab." Travis assured him.

"A tab you don't pay." Ian clarified, earning him a wide grin.

Ian rolled his eyes and walked to the counter. Jeremiah swiped Ian's credit card and waited as he signed. "Hey Jer," Travis began, "meet my new roommate, Ian O'Dell. He'll probably be around more often."

Jeremiah shook Ian's hand. "Nice to hear you finally found someone willing to live with you."

"Oh man, what does he mean by that?" Ian turned to Travis with regret and Jeremiah laughed.

"Kidding man, Travis is a good guy. Just giving him a hard time. Besides, anyone who is willing to live across the street from Kat must be sent from God."

Ian's brow furrowed as he turned to Travis yet again. Travis slapped him on the back. "He's kidding." But Ian did not miss the sharp glare Travis shot towards a smirking Jeremiah as they turned to leave.

"How about you bring a load over on your way tomorrow?" Travis asked, as he slid behind the wheel of their police cruiser.

"I could do that. I don't have much in the way of furniture."

"No worries. Most of the house is furnished other than the two bedrooms that will be yours."

"Good deal." Ian buckled his seat belt as Travis pulled away from the curb. Glancing once more at the café, Ian felt a slight edge to his nerves about helping Travis at Kat's house the following morning.

∞

Kat awoke to the smell of freshly brewed coffee and allowed the scent to nudge her feet down the hallway and into the small kitchen where Sara sat at the bar scrolling through her phone. "Travis is coming over and bringing his new roommate to help." She announced without glancing up.

Kat poured a cup of coffee into her favorite polka dot mug. "Roommate? He found one?"

Chicago's Best

"Yep. Yesterday apparently."

"Who is it?"

"He didn't say. Said it was a surprise."

"I hate surprises."

"I love surprises." Sara countered. "Besides, it's Travis, I'm sure he considered us when deciding."

Kat shrugged as if the matter did not bother her. "I was going to dart to the café this morning and make sure the crescent dough is pliable."

"What? No." Sara firmly placed her hands on her hips. "If you go up to the café you will not be back for hours and we will be right where we are now on painting the rest of the house. Jeremiah can see to the dough."

"He doesn't make the dough. I do." Kat countered.

Sara went back to her phone and held it to her ear. "Hey Jer Bear. So, Kat needs to know if the crescent dough is pliable?" She paused as if listening. "Uh huh, you guessed it." She covered the mouthpiece. "He's onto you as well."

Kat looked at her innocently.

"Yes, she's trying to get out of painting."

"Not true," Kat called out so Jeremiah could hear her.

"He says the dough is fine and that you are free to help me all day."

"I don't know about all day, but okay, I give in. I will not go to the café this morning."

"Good." Sara hung up her phone and a smile slipped over her face as she heard the front door open.

"Hello, hello!" Travis called from the living room.

Sara hopped off her stool and darted into the other room, her squeal of pleasure loud enough that Kat heard it from the kitchen. She grinned to herself; though the two lovebirds sometimes annoyed her, she still found their affection sweet at times. She grabbed a bagel and made her way towards the living room with her coffee. Her eyes widened in surprise as Ian O'Dell stood next to Travis, freshly showered and looking gorgeous. *He was tall*, she realized. *Really tall.* And her eyes roamed over the muscular biceps that peeked out of his shirtsleeves. She fidgeted as all eyes turned towards her as she mentally kicked herself for not applying her make up.

"Mornin', Kat." Travis greeted. "Anymore coffee?"

She motioned over her shoulder. "Yep. Help yourself."

"Good morning, Kat Riesling." Ian greeted. "Like the wine."

She couldn't help the smile that tugged at her lips. "Morning, Oscar... I mean, Ian. You clean up nicely."

He looked down at his jeans and t-shirt. "Thanks."

"Wish he could say the same to you." Travis nudged her on his way to the kitchen as he tousled her bed head.

"I haven't gotten ready for the day just yet." Kat defended. "That takes at least my first cup of coffee." Though she played off Travis' comment with ease, she could not help the small flush of embarrassment that crept up her neck. She found Ian watching her and she flushed even further. Setting her mug on the sofa side table, she motioned towards the hallway. "I think I will quickly go make myself presentable."

"You look fine." Ian stated.

Pausing, Kat turned towards him in surprise. The pink to his cheeks told her he was not expecting to toss out the compliment. "Thanks, but I think I should put on some clothes I don't mind getting paint on. Be back in a few. Oh, and feel free to help yourself to some coffee in the kitchen."

Ian watched her leave.

"Ahem."

He turned to find Sara still in the living room watching him. He flushed. "Nice to meet you, Sara, I am assuming." He extended his hand and she shook it. "You must be Travis' new detective partner."

"Yes."

"And roommate." Travis added walking back into the room and handing Ian a cup of coffee.

"I see." Sara linked her arm with Ian's. "May God have mercy on your soul." She giggled as Travis reached towards her and pinched her arm playfully.

Kat walked back down the hallway. "I think I'm going to have to take Kissa to the vet this week. That scratch on my ankle looks like it may have an infection."

"So you think Kissa has what, some sort of disease?" Travis asked on a laugh.

"I don't know. That's why I should probably take her."

"Did you disinfect the scratch when it happened?" Ian asked.

"No. Well, not right away." Kat admitted. "I didn't think much of it, to be honest. I've never had cats before and just thought it was nothing. But it's really starting to burn."

"You can get sick from even a small scratch." Ian continued. "Do you feel feverish?" He placed the back of his hand on her forehead, Kat taking a step back at the contact. He nervously shoved his hand back into his jean's pocket. "Apologies."

"I feel fine." She stated. "But thanks."

He nodded, the awkwardness in the room almost his undoing.

"So." Travis clapped his hands and grinned. "Where did you ladies want to start painting?"

Both women pointed to the wall housing the small stone fireplace.

"And what color did you guys finally decide upon?" Travis perused the various paint cans and grimaced at several as he passed by.

"The mint color." Sara picked up a can and handed it to him with a smile.

"Mint-to-be." Kat corrected.

Sara rolled her eyes. "Of course, 'mint-to-be', Ms. Technicalities."

"And what about the kitchen?" He asked.

"That is my area." Kat interjected. "I chose the always beautiful, lavender, excuse me, I mean Lavender Plush." She pulled aside her paint can.

"So, basically every room is to be a different color?" Travis asked.

"Exactly." Both women replied.

Ian smiled as he reached for the lavender paint in Kat's hand.

"You helping me in the kitchen?" Kat asked in surprise.

"I thought I might." Ian shoved his other hand in his jean pocket. "Unless you'd rather paint in there alone."

"I would never turn down help." Kat grinned and turned towards the kitchen.

"Good luck." Travis called after him. "She's a perfectionist."

Kat popped her head around the corner wall. "I'm neat, not a perfectionist, Trav. There's a difference. Now don't get paint on the stones." She pointed towards the fireplace before popping her head back into the kitchen.

«CHAPTER TWO»

IAN SET THE PAINT can on the bar top and admired the bright room. Though small, the kitchen held a charm to it that Kat seemed to appreciate as she began taping off the edges of the walls. "Nice space."

She looked up with a genuine smile. "Thanks. It's part of the reason I wanted to buy the house. I sort of envision its former life somewhere in the countryside of France."

"Former life?" He asked in amusement.

She continued pulling the blue paint tape alongside the cabinet. "A country cottage that sits upon rolling hills of the French countryside with wild wisteria and irises swaying in the pleasant breeze and a full garden of fresh vegetables just ripe for the picking."

"You've given it a lot of thought."

She turned towards him and tossed him a roll of blue tape. "I'm a dreamer, what can I say?"

He began unrolling the tape and applying it to the opposite corner of the wall.

"As close as you can get it to the corner and as straight as possible. I don't like sloppy paint jobs."

He nodded. "I think I can handle it."

She watched him for several seconds, and though his back faced her, he could feel the weight of her scrutiny.

"What's your story, Ian?" She asked, before turning back to her own work. "How long have you been a detective?"

"Going on six years now."

"And have you always worked here in Chicago? Because I don't think I've ever heard Travis mention you."

"No. I transferred from a precinct out of New York a few months ago."

"New York. Nice." She climbed on top of a stool and pulled a piece of tape tight up towards the ceiling. "I'm not a big fan of New York, myself, but I admire people who are willing to live there."

"What do you not like about it?"

"It's dirty."

"And Chicago isn't?" He chuckled.

"Only some parts of Chicago are dirty." Kat explained.

"Same in New York."

"Not that I saw."

"Well, then maybe you didn't see enough of the city." He countered with a slight defensive tone that had her turning to face him.

She smirked. "Maybe so." She turned back to her task. "What made you leave?"

"It was dirty."

She stopped what she was doing and turned to see that his face was serious and then she started laughing. "Oh really?"

He grinned, and she realized his easy smile was charming and the slight appearance of a dimple in his left cheek made him seem less intimidating than before. Shrugging, he turned back to his work.

"Gato, Chat, and Kissa?"

"What about them?" She asked, as she moved her stool a few feet over and climbed up again. Ian watched as she balanced herself against the wall as she tore off a piece of tape.

"They all have the same name."

"Yep."

"But in different languages."

"Yep."

He rubbed a hand over his face as if struggling with patience at her clipped answers. "Why name them all "cat" in different languages?"

"I thought it was a fun idea. That and my name is Kat, so we are just a bunch of cats at the café." She smiled over her shoulder. "I'm impressed you knew their names were all the same."

"I'm fluent in French. I know some Spanish. And I've only come across one other person in my life that knows Finnish, so I found it interesting. Are you gifted in these languages as well?"

"Fluent in French as well." She smiled. "A little Spanish, and I spent two years abroad in Finland."

"Impressive." He earned the light blush that crossed her face before she turned back towards the tape roll in her hands.

"I never thanked you." She looked up, her gaze serious as she surveyed him.

"For what?"

"For catching the thugs that hoped to bring drugs to our side of the city, and for protecting my café... and my cats." She smirked as he chuckled.

"It's what we do."

"I do believe you are the first police officer I've ever seen hide in a city dumpster for hours on end."

"Yeah, I think I drew the short straw on that one."

"It's admirable, though. And does not go unnoticed." She walked over to the paint bucket and tray. "I think we are ready to paint the walls."

"You don't want to double check my taping skills?"

"Very funny. But no. I trust your abilities." Kat poured paint into the tray, the pale purple a nice contrast against the white cabinets and slate countertops. "I'll edge if you roll." She handed him the paint roller.

"I can definitely do that." He reached for the roller as the doorbell rang and Kat walked to the edge of the room as she peeked around the corner.

Travis opened the door and his defensive stance told her exactly who stood on the other side.

"Kat!" He called over his shoulder. "It's for you!"

She groaned as she set her paintbrush down on the counter. "Be right back." She marched out of the kitchen with a storm in her eyes and Ian feared for the person awaiting her wrath. Curiosity had him stepping towards the open doorway of the kitchen to look. Travis caught his eye as Kat greeted the man on the front stoop.

"Marshall? What are you doing here?"

Ian mouthed 'Thompson?' towards Travis and he nodded. Ian's brow furrowed as he contemplated the multiple reasons why Kat would have dealings with the city's most renowned attorney.

"I came to see you. I heard about the arrests outside your café. I wanted to make sure you were alright."

"Really?" Kat asked in disbelief.

A hand reached out and slid from her elbow to her hand and Kat quickly shrugged it away. "Of course, Kat. You know I still have feelings for you."

"Um, no, I don't. And I really don't think it matters even if you did. Thanks for coming by, Marshall, but it was completely unnecessary. Now if you'll excuse me..." She reached to close the door and his hand shot out, forcefully holding it against the wall. Ian jerked to attention the same time Travis did and both men entered the living room as Marshall Thompson stepped into the house. Marshall's steel gaze met Ian's and his left brow quirked. "I apologize, Kat, I did not realize you had company." He stepped forward and extended his hand. Ian glanced down at it and hesitated before clasping it in his own. "So, you must be him." Marshall continued.

Kat reached Ian's side and glowered at Marshall as she crossed her arms over her chest. "He is none of your concern, Marshall. Now I think it is time for you to leave."

"Oh come now, Kat. Do I not at least receive the courtesy of meeting your new boyfriend?"

"He is not my boyfriend," she corrected and Marshall's smile broadened. "Not like it is any of your business." She reached out and turned Marshall's shoulders towards the door. "Now go."

Snickering, Marshall turned to face her on the stoop as he stepped outside. "I hated to hear that your safety was in jeopardy, Kat."

"Why? I'm sure they are just your next clients anyway."

Marshall sneered. "Actually, no. Once again, I have nothing to do with the drug problem in this city. I thought I had proven that to you."

She leaned against the doorway as he reached a hand out and attempted to brush his knuckles down her cheek. She swatted his hand away.

"You will miss me, Kat. One day you will miss me and I will have moved on. Are you sure you want to turn me away?"

Ian looked to Travis as he made his way towards the door to stand behind Kat as Marshall Thompson baited her with smooth words.

"I find that hard to believe, so my answer is still the same. Goodbye, Marshall." She slammed the door and turned only to bump into Ian's chest. He gripped her arms to stabilize her as she swiped a loose strand of hair out of her eyes.

"Thanks." She stepped around him and headed back to the kitchen.

"You will need to explain all this to me later," Ian muttered to Travis.

"You got it." Travis nodded for Ian to make his way back to the kitchen.

Kat swished the brush from the corner of the room near the ceiling and along the tapeline. She felt Ian step back into the room before she even saw him, and she waited for the question everyone asked her when it came to Marshall.

"So how do you know Marshall Thompson?" Ian asked.

And there it was, she thought. She dipped her brush back in her cup and continued painting.

"Talk and paint, O'Dell, that's the deal."

She heard him shuffling around behind her and then the smooth sound of roller on wall. *Good, at least he wasn't going to leave her to do all the painting. Yet.*

"He's my ex." The smooth sound stopped and she waited a breath before continuing. "It's been over about a year, but he still seems to believe I will just change my mind one day."

"And why did it end?"

"Um, have you met the man?" she asked.

Ian noticed her shoulders tense as she shifted to paint another spot along the wall. "I apologize."

She turned to him in confusion.

"It's none of my business," he confessed.

"You're right, it's not," she replied, but then a tender smile washed over her face. "And thank you, for saying that. Most people want to keep prying once they find out I dated the most evil man in the city. Trust me, at the time, I did not know he was as vile as he is."

"What made you realize his lack of character?"

He assumed he passed whatever test she was giving him as she studied him carefully before responding. "Honestly," she sighed. "Not one thing in particular. I just... had a bad feeling in my gut. And I always listen to my gut." She held a fist in front of her midsection as if demonstrating the fierce loyalty she had with her discernment. "Then other events and happenings did not add up, and I noticed the company he started keeping, the clients he represented. If Marshall was not involved in the drug rings around Chicago, he at least was being threatened by them. Why else would he represent some of those men? And why push to have their charges dropped or jail time decreased? He had to be in someone's pocket or he was threatened."

"You truly believed your boyfriend to be a criminal?"

"At first, no. But even I cannot be blind to what was before me. He started to change. And I realized that it was not fear that drove him to succeed or take the cases he did. He thrived on it. He loved beating the system. He loved cheating the system. When I confronted him-"

"You confronted him?!" Ian's voice rose in surprise.

"Of course. Wouldn't you?"

Ian waved for her to continue.

"He denied any wrongdoing of course, but then the very next day a couple of thugs stormed into my café and tossed me around a little bit and threatened me."

"They what?" He stepped forward as if defending her honor and a soft smile tilted her lips.

"I got the message loud and clear. Marshall was in their circle and should I push or say anything about him then I would be at risk. Thankfully, I truly did not know anything as far as specifics, and it took a while for Marshall to understand that. But once he did, the threats stopped. The surprise visits stopped. Until today."

"Until a drug bust just happened to occur behind your café." He finished for her.

"Exactly. So his visit here tonight was not out of concern for me, it was concern for himself, I'm sure, or the men that were arrested. He wanted to remind me of my place and of what could happen should I cause problems."

"I see." He turned back to the wall and painted.

"Do you believe me?" She asked.

"Yes."

"Just like that?" She snapped her fingers and he faced her once more.

"Why wouldn't I?"

"Not many people do. Some believe I knew all along how shady he was… or is, for that matter."

"If you knew then, what does it matter now? You separated yourself from him." He saw the disappointment wash over her face. "But for what it's worth, I do believe you knew nothing about his escapades."

"Thanks."

He shrugged. "Don't thank me yet. I have a feeling this is all just beginning. His presence here tonight makes me wonder if you will receive more visits in the near future. I will be at your café tomorrow just in case."

"Staking it out?"

"Yes. Because like you, I'm interested in who Marshall represents and interacts with."

"I'm not interested anymore." She corrected. "If he is trying to bring crime to this end of the city, then I want it stopped. I could care less how much control or authority Marshall has in this city. He needs to be handled."

"Well, thank you for trusting me with your story. I am sure it is not easy to tell."

"For some reason, it is with you."

He smiled.

"Don't make me regret it." She held out her paintbrush to enforce her point and he laughed.

"You got it."

∞

Kat unlocked the door to the café. The early morning quiet washed over her and calmed her frazzled nerves. She felt someone watching. *Crazy*, she thought, *considering it's 4:45 in the morning.* But still, she felt uneasy. She quickly turned her key and flipped on the nearest light switch and gasped at what stood before her. Blue paint covered her entryway, followed by portraits of her face from her recent newspaper interview. "Snitch" graced the floor and posters. She fumbled with her cell phone and dialed Travis.

"Café. Now. Emergency." She hung up and ran towards the kitchen, locking herself inside. She dialed Jeremiah. Living in the upstairs loft, he knocked on the back door within seconds and she let him in.

"Are you okay?" He gripped her shoulders and then pulled her into a tight hug and felt her nod against his shoulder.

Pulling away, Kat tried to hide the shakiness of her hands by reaching for her apron and tying it around her. "Travis is on his way."

"Good. This has to be in response to yesterday's bust. Have you talked to Sara this morning? Did her shop get broken into as well?"

"I have no idea." Kat looked at her watch. "She won't be there for another hour, so she may not know yet."

Kat's cell phone rang. Travis.

"Hey, we're at the front door. You can come out now."

She stepped from the kitchen, Jeremiah following close behind. Several officers patrolled the café, snapping photos, writing notes, but one stood outside barking orders. Ian. She followed him with her gaze until he looked up and found her staring. She did not divert her gaze as relief swept over her as he marched towards her. "You okay?" He reached towards her and she found herself comforted by his embrace. *When did this happen?* She wondered. She relished the security before stepping back and looking into his intense eyes. "I'm fine. Just a bit shaken up."

He rubbed warmth back into her arms as he looked over to Travis. "The glass door at the alternate entrance was the point of entry. Do you not have an alarm system?"

She nodded. "It wasn't on when I got here though, so they must have disabled it somehow."

"Who all knows how to disarm it?"

Kat motioned between herself and Jeremiah. "Just us two."

Ian stared hard at Jeremiah.

"Travis told me you live upstairs?"

"That's right." Jeremiah shoved his hands into his pockets.

"And you didn't hear anything last night or this morning?"

"Not a thing. But I usually sleep with the television on."

"And did you last night?"

"Yes."

"What was the last show you watched?"

Jeremiah shifted uncomfortably. Kat linked her arm in his. "It wasn't Jeremiah, Ian."

"I still need an answer to the question." Ian waited, his stance patient, but his eyes remained hard.

"The Walking Dead. There was a marathon going. I'm not sure which episode off the top of my head."

Ian eyed him closely, obvious dissatisfaction settled over his features. Kat stepped forward and lightly laid her hand on Ian's arm. "It wasn't Jeremiah, and he did not have anything to do with it. Trust me."

Ian looked down into Kat's face and nodded. "Fine. But I may have more questions later on."

"That's fine." Jeremiah said, as he looked towards the doorway. "We better put a sign up or something Kat, because we will be having our early birds in about a half hour."

"Let them come. The paint is still wet. The posters are being taken down already. I'll find a piece of wood to block the broken door window and call to have that replaced. I'm not closing up shop because some loser decided to break into my business."

"But you haven't started baking anything." Jeremiah looked to the clock in apprehension.

"I'll have something ready. If I can get to it?" She looked to Ian for dismissal and he nodded. She tossed a small wave across the room to Travis as she headed for the kitchen.

"I seriously did not hear a thing last night." Jeremiah restated for Ian. "But I can say that I will be more vigilant. Kat's... well she is special to me. I don't want anything to happen to her."

Ian watched as Jeremiah turned and headed for the counter to start coffee in the various machines. He wondered what Jeremiah meant about Kat being special to him. *Were they involved? Did Jeremiah wish to be involved with her? Would he pull off a stunt like this to draw Kat into his arms for comfort?*

"If you stare at that door any harder a hole will burn through." Travis observed as he stepped up next to Ian pulling off a set of rubber gloves. "I think we are done here for now. Kat's got a cleanup crew coming to take care of the paint. I'm going to head next door and make sure the flower shop didn't have any vandalism issues. Sara hasn't shown up yet, but I have a key. Want to join?"

"What is Jeremiah's relationship with Kat?" Ian asked, causing Travis's brows to disappear into his hairline.

"Jeremiah? Why?"

"I want to know." Ian stated plainly.

"Are you asking professionally speaking or for personal reasons?" Travis asked with a tilt to his lips and a glint in his eye.

"Professional reasons."

"Right." Travis began walking towards the door and Ian followed. "He and Kat are friends. Close friends. He is actually part of our small group of friends. Kat, Sara, Jeremiah, and me. He's worked at the café for the last three years, lived upstairs majority of that time."

"Does he have a record?"

"Not that I know of."

"You've never checked?"

"Do you check all your friends' priors?" Travis countered in defense. "Didn't think so. I can positively say it is not Jeremiah, now can we move on or would you like to keep wasting time?"

Ian took a deep breath and dropped the subject as he headed to the door to leave.

"Wait!" Kat called, darting out of the kitchen carrying a bright green box and sliding across the slick floor to stop in front of them. She grinned. "Here." She handed the box to Travis. "For the both of you. It was an early morning and I owe you."

She patted Ian on the shoulder and darted back to the kitchen.

"Breakfast." Travis held up the box. "Let's go."

∞

Kat waited until she heard the last of the officers leave and then ventured out into the main dining area. Jeremiah watched as she surveyed the damage.

"It's really not that bad," she stated. "I think the cleanup crew will be able to erase it all."

"Good thing neither of us was here when it happened." He crossed his arms over his chest. "Travis told me Marshall visited you last night. Think it was him?"

"No." Kat sighed as she sat in a chair at one of the front tables and Jeremiah took the one opposite her. "Though I do have a feeling he's involved somehow. I mean, I haven't seen or spoken to Marshall in months and all of a sudden after the bust he shows up at my door and then this." She motioned around the room. "I don't think that is a coincidence."

"So what do you want to do?" Jeremiah asked.

"Besides kick him in the pants?"

He laughed and then grimaced making her giggle.

"I don't think there is really anything I can do. Though I will say I am not the snitch. That was Sara's doing."

"Stupid Sara." Jeremiah joked.

"For real." Kat agreed on a laugh. "If her flower shop was untouched, I'm going to make her deliver fresh flowers for the tables the next two weeks."

"You should." Jeremiah stood and pushed his chair in. "By the way, the new guy..."

"What about him?"

"Travis said he was going to be his roommate as well as his new partner at work. Is he always that serious?"

"I don't know. I just met him yesterday during the bust and then he helped us paint for a while last night. He seems nice enough. But yeah, a bit serious. I think he is just trying to take it all in, you know? I mean, we can be a lot to handle."

"Don't I know it." Jeremiah pulled her ponytail in brotherly affection as he headed towards the counter.

"You're still my favorite!" Kat called after him. Jeremiah acknowledged her with a wave over his shoulder and she smiled.

«CHAPTER THREE»

KAT KNEW IT WAS only a matter of time before Sara came busting into her kitchen. What she had hoped was that it would not be in the middle of her lunch rush. However, Sara had always had a flare for the dramatics, and Kat acknowledged her with a swift glance as Sara burst through the back door of the café and straight into the kitchen.

"I cannot believe you are open today after what happened this morning!" She plopped herself down on one of the stools at the metal work table and watched as Kat finished the touches on two plates before setting them on a serving tray. Amy, a college student and one of Kat's waitresses, buzzed inside and grabbed the tray and hustled back out.

"I still have to make a living," Kat said as she wiped her hands on a dishtowel and eased down onto a stool opposite Sara. Sara reached across the table and squeezed her hand. "I'm so sorry, Kat. I did not even think about something like this happening in response to my informing Travis of the strange men."

"You have no reason to apologize." Kat squeezed Sara's hand and then stood as Jeremiah walked in and laid two order slips on the counter and walked back out. As Kat began prepping the dishes, Sara reached into her purse and pulled out a handheld mirror and lightly teased her blonde hair with her fingers and ran a fingertip around her lips to clean her latest lipstick application. Sara had been Kat's best friend since middle school. The sprightly blonde with the bright blue eyes housed a keen mind for business, though she sometimes hid her smarts behind her beautiful smile and flirtatious lashes. She and Kat had bought their house last year, both pitching in half in order to stake their claim on a piece of property outside the city. The small, quaint cottage fit Kat perfectly, but Sara had her eye on another house. The one across the street. Travis' house. Kat knew it was only a matter of time before her two friends tied the knot, but Sara could not stand not having Kat nearby. So they bought the house so they could all continue to be neighbors when the time for wedding bells came. Kat placed the next two orders on trays and Jeremiah buzzed in and turned back out.

"You guys have such a system." Sara complimented.

"It's the lunch rush. Speed is important." Kat sat back down and glanced at her watch. "We're in the last 30 minutes now though, and then it will slow a bit. So, did anything happen to your store last night?"

Sara shook her head. "Thankfully, no. But Travis said he would have an unmarked surveillance officer parked across the street for our shops tonight. Hopefully neither of us will have any further issues."

"I plan on crashing here tonight to make sure of it." Kat crossed her arms in preparedness for Sara's argument.

"Here? As in your café? Where? You no longer have the loft upstairs now that Jeremiah lives there."

"I have the cot in my office." Kat motioned towards the back.

"A cot?!" Sara asked in horror. "No. It is not safe for you stay here at night by yourself."

"There will be a surveillance officer outside all night. You said so yourself."

"But-" Sara trailed off as Kat held up her hand.

"Look, Sara, I have to do this. Besides, I've stayed here at night before and everything has gone fine. I just want to make sure the new security system operates well and that I feel safe. I work late most nights, so I need to feel safe. This is a test run to see if I will feel that way."

"Travis is not going to like this," Sara warned.

"He will have to." As Kat finished her sentence, Travis walked into the room through the swinging door leading to the main dining area. "Um, customers are not allowed back here," Kat teased, as she stood to intercept order slips from Amy.

"Just came to check on you. Any other disturbances today?"

"Nope. Perfectly safe. New security system should be rockin' and rollin' in another hour or so, and then I will be good to go." Kat smiled. "Thanks for coming so fast this morning."

"That was O'Dell's doing. He drove like greased lightning."

Kat's right brow rose in curiosity at that tidbit of information before placing a dish on a tray.

"Kat plans on sleeping up here tonight," she heard Sara whisper to Travis and she bristled with annoyance.

"What?" His voice slightly rose as he made eye contact with Kat. "You can't be serious?"

"Serious as a heart attack," Kat clarified. "I've already explained my reasoning to Sara, and Jeremiah is just upstairs if I get scared. I will be fine. Plus, imagine what all I can accomplish in an all-nighter."

"I don't like it." Travis leaned against the doorway. "O'Dell isn't going to like it either."

"What would it matter if O'Dell likes it or not?" Kat asked in offense that another person had a say in her life.

"Because he's one of the detectives on the case, Kat. Your café was targeted just this morning with a direct threat spelled out for you. Your safety is compromised here." Travis explained.

"And Sara informed me you guys will have a guard out front all night long. I have Jeremiah. I have my wits. I'll be fine. If I hear or feel anything suspicious or scary, I will call. Just like I did this morning." Kat glanced up as the door opened once more and Jeremiah poked his head in. "Kat, the new guy wants to talk to you." He motioned over his shoulder and ducked back out.

"New guy?" She wondered aloud as she stepped through the door and Ian waited patiently by the counter. "Well, well, well... look who has manners." She smiled in welcome. "Unlike two other people I know." She squinted a phony glare at Travis and Sara before turning back towards Ian. "What can I do for you, Detective O'Dell?"

"You can call me Ian." He stated, before he reached into his back pocket and pulled out a photo. "Have you ever seen this man?"

Kat studied the face of the young man in the photo. Nothing about his face rang a bell. "No. I don't think so."

He frowned and shoved it back into his pocket. "Have you seen anyone today out of the ordinary? New customer? Anyone suspicious?"

She shook her head. "No. Though I've spent almost all day in the back except this morning while you guys were here after the incident."

Disappointment washed over his face as he nodded. "Well keep your eyes open-" his words were cut off by the sound of shattering glass and customer screams. Ian hopped the counter and tackled Kat to the ground, covering her with his body. She tried to nudge him aside, but he remained solid as Travis emerged from the kitchen and looked down at them. "What happened?"

Ian shrugged. "Not sure yet."

Travis looked around at the chaos as people rushed to leave, and those remaining circled around objects on the floor. Several bricks dotted the floor as Ian finally stood up and helped Kat to her feet. Her gaze fluttered about the room and she cringed. She looked to a wide-eyed Jeremiah. "Flip the sign. We're closed." He quickly walked to the front entrance and changed the sign as Kat stood on a chair and clapped her hands.

"Everyone! Everyone!" She called for attention and customers turned to face her and the mumbles died down. "I am terribly sorry for the intrusion on your lunchtime. I am afraid we will be closing for the remainder of the day, but if you give me about five minutes I will have portable lunches for you to take with you, on the house." She nodded towards Jeremiah as he darted into the kitchen and began working on meals and Amy followed behind him. She climbed down and placed her hands on her narrow hips.

"Well?"

Ian ended a phone call and looked up. "Rogers saw two men throw the bricks. He set out on foot after them, but lost them at the traffic light on 4th and Lexington. I've got Smithens checking traffic cams and security camera footage as we speak. We need to get these people out of here."

Travis nodded. "On it." He watched as Jeremiah and Amy emerged carrying boxed lunches and handing them to people as they exited. Most customers were unperturbed by the event and more remorseful towards Kat for having to deal with the mess. For that, she was grateful. Sighing, she walked into the kitchen and came back with a broom, followed by a hysterical Sara. Sara ran to Travis and flung herself into his arms. Kat rolled her eyes before starting to sweep.

"Wait." Ian snatched the broom away and she turned with eyes full of temper. "We have to take some photographs first."

Her shoulders deflated and she eased into a chair. Two patrol cars pulled up outside and officers began spilling into the café and setting to work on clearing the scene. Kat watched in a daze as her café was invaded. Jeremiah sat across from her and grabbed her hands. "I sent Amy home and all customers are gone. Most of them actually paid their tab before leaving so there's a perk."

Kat's mouth tilted into an appreciative smile at his efforts to cheer her up. Ian walked up, his eyes surveying their joined hands before finding her face. "Our team is finished now."

Kat nodded and began to stand as a voice filtered through the room. "I don't care who you are, I am Ms. Riesling's attorney." Kat looked up and Ian turned to see Marshall Thompson stomping through the café towards them. He reached for Kat and she backed up. "I cannot believe this, Kat. Are you alright? No one was hurt, were they?"

"What are you doing here, Marshall?" Kat asked, wishing Ian would walk away instead of studying her with his intense gaze.

"I was headed here for lunch when I saw the patrol cars out front and people rushing to leave. What on Earth happened?" He looked around at the mess, but his eyes did not hold concern. His demeanor too relaxed for him to be full of such worry. *False sense of care,* Ian thought.

"I appreciate you checking on me, but everything is fine. Just a couple of thugs up to no good. The police are looking into it."

"This is the second time today and their attacks keep escalating. What exactly are you doing to keep Kat safe?" Marshall challenged Ian.

"For starters, Mr. Thompson, we are clearing the café." He inserted himself between Kat and Marshall and began walking towards Marshall to encourage him to start walking away. Marshall glowered as he tried to speak to Kat once more. "I will come by tonight, Kat, after work. We can discuss this further."

"There's nothing to discuss, Marshall," Kat said, as she walked beside Ian and Marshall reached the door. "The only thing I need from you is for you to tell Biggs, or whoever is sending these thugs, to please stop. I don't take kindly to threats, especially when I have done nothing wrong."

"What makes you think this was Biggs? And why on Earth would you think I have a connection to him?" Marshall asked.

"You were the attorney for three of his men last Fall. I'm sure you maintained some connections."

"And you think he did this? Why?"

She shrugged. "The only drug ring I know of is his. That sort of narrows it down." She crossed her arms over her chest as Marshall took a deep breath.

"If you need me, you know where to find me." He turned and left.

∞

Kat exhaled loudly and sank back into a chair. "This is all so crazy." She braced her elbows on the table and covered her face in her hands before dragging them through her hair.

"O'Dell." Travis walked up and motioned over his shoulder. "What was Thompson doing here?"

Ian looked back to Kat and she shrugged.

"Pretending to care." Kat said.

"So he shows up last night at your house, and now he shows up here after the two incidents? Do you think that is coincidence?" Travis asked her in a scolding manner.

"Don't take that tone with me." Kat pointed a finger in his chest. "I'm not stupid. Of course he is connected to this all somehow. I'm not blind. I just don't want to think about it at the moment. I have bigger fish to fry." She motioned to the mess she still needed to clean up. "It's your job to find the connection, is it not?"

"I'm trying to," Travis defended. "But I need to make sure I have all the facts. If you are secretly back with Marshall or have been communicating with him recently, I need to know."

"What?!" Kat's eyes bulged in shock. "No, I am not seeing Marshall! Are you kidding me?"

"I have to ask, Kat."

"No you don't," she challenged. "You should know me better than that."

Travis squeezed her shoulder. "I was just making sure. I did not mean to sound accusatory. But it is suspicious."

Kat gawked at him before storming away and grabbing the broom to begin sweeping.

"Nice job." Ian mumbled.

"Hey, one of us had to ask, and since you were just standing there..." Travis muttered.

"I was watching her reactions to your questions."

"And?"

"She isn't seeing Marshall Thompson. She was just as surprised as us when he walked inside, and when he spoke to her, she was genuinely unimpressed."

"So what do you think we need to do?" Travis watched as a team began placing boards in the windows and Kat and Jeremiah cleaned up the glass while other officers straightened tables and chairs.

"Not sure. It does not make sense for Kat to be targeted for simply reporting suspicious activity."

"Activity she really didn't even report. It was Sara. I can understand the attack this morning. They thought she ratted them out. But this one? During business hours? This is a statement. But why make a statement to Kat?"

"Maybe the message is not aimed at Kat. Maybe someone else." He nodded towards the doorway and they both watched Marshall Thompson as he stood near his car watching the scene. "Perhaps Thompson is in hot water with Biggs, and this is Biggs' way of sending a warning."

"What? That he will attack those he cares about?" Travis asked.

"Yes, or those closest to him."

"But Kat hasn't had anything to do with him since last Fall."

"But does Biggs know that?" Ian asked. "Kat mentioned something about Marshall representing three of his minions last Fall. Maybe it has something to do with that."

"I'll dig up the case and see what the three were charged with and their connection to Biggs and Marshall." Travis made a note and stuffed the notepad back into his pocket. "She recognize the photo you showed her?"

"No."

"So that rules out Traveler's drug ring."

"Yep."

"So we are definitely looking at Biggs. If you think about it, it makes perfect sense. Traveler starts taking over the West side of the city, Biggs' territory. Biggs starts infiltrating this way to expand, but it's not as easy to accomplish as he thought."

Ian rubbed a hand over his chin. "What if Thompson not only represented Biggs' men, but began representing Traveler's men as well? That would certainly upset Biggs, and could have started a small war and put Thompson in hot water."

"True. Definitely something to look into. I'll see if we can get a run down of all Thompson's court cases from the last year." Travis made another note. "I think that about sums it up here for now. Kat's closing for the rest of the day, though earlier she mentioned staying here tonight."

"Staying here? All night?" Ian asked.

"Yep. She wants to make sure the new security system works well and she wants to get some work done. She's pulled all-nighters in the past, but I specifically told her it was too dangerous for her to do it tonight. She wasn't listening. She thinks with Jeremiah and the officer out front she will be safe enough."

"And does she believe that now?" Ian waved a hand over the café's dining area.

"I don't know. Probably. Once she makes up her mind, it is hard to convince her otherwise. If we had the manpower I would assign a bodyguard to her. She's clearly being targeted, but we just can't stretch the coverage right now." The two men watched as Kat dumped a dustpan full of shards of glass into a giant trashcan. She looked up and forced a smile.

"Good thing the window guy was already on his way," she commented. "Looks like all my broken windows will be replaced by the end of the day, and I'll be back up and running tomorrow."

"If you have customers." Travis blurted before thinking and received two sharp slaps upside the head, one from Kat and one from Ian. Kat grinned at the temporary teamwork with Ian. "Ian and I were just discussing your plans to stay here tonight," Travis continued.

"Good. I definitely have my work cut out for me now since I lost half a day's business today. I may call in several extra hands tomorrow to do intersection sales in the morning."

"Intersection sales?" Ian asked.

"Sometimes I have people standing at busy intersections with a small table of packaged baked goods so people can grab them on the way to work."

He considered her idea and nodded.

"We do not think you should stay here tonight," Travis stated. "Besides, Sara would be upset and scared for you."

"She's scared for herself at home, Trav. We both know her worry is not all aimed towards me." Kat corrected. "And I have to work tonight if I'm going to have enough bagged and boxed pastries for in the morning."

"You were attacked twice today, Kat!" Travis ran a hand through his dark hair, his deep brown eyes sharp. "Surely you can see that it is not a smart idea."

"Then give me an officer to watch over me."

"I can't. We are shorthanded already. We cannot give you a personal detail right now."

"I'll do it." Ian stepped forward and had them both surveying him. Kat with a smile and Travis with a frown.

"You'll do it?" Travis asked.

"Yes. If she wants to stay here and work, she needs protection. My shift ends at six, I will come by afterwards." Ian spread his hands in question to see if that worked for Kat. She all but danced in place as she ran towards him and hugged him tightly.

"Thank you, thank you, thank you!" She kissed his cheek with a loud smack of her lips. Squeezing him one more time before she darted towards the kitchen.

"Really?" Travis asked, his annoyance evident as he shook his head.

"Look, we both know she would have come back up here even if I did not offer. At least this way she has coverage inside as well as out." Ian explained.

Travis pondered his reasoning for a moment. "You're probably right. Then I am going to have Sara stay at our place tonight just in case something happens at their house tonight."

"Sounds good." Ian walked towards the kitchen and knocked on the door.

Kat pushed it back and smiled. "I just love that you don't barge in. What's up?"

"We are headed back to the station. Officer Craig is out front if you need him. I will return about six."

"Thank you again, Ian. You have no idea how much I appreciate it."

He studied her soft face for a moment, the creamy brown eyes full of gratitude and he felt something inside him soften.

"O'Dell! You coming?!" Travis called from the door.

Ian stepped away from Kat. "See you at six." He turned and made his way out the door feeling Kat's gaze on his back the entire way.

∞

Kat glanced up at the clock on her kitchen wall as she continued to grate cheese. The movement calmed her, the slight drag down the grate that left fluffy yellow shreds of cheese in its wake. Kat loved the simple chore of grating cheese. She loved it more when she had the entire café to herself, and the quiet work of prepping for tomorrow left her feeling rejuvenated after the stressful day. She had sent Jeremiah home, though that was just upstairs. He promised to be next to his phone in case she needed him. She glanced at the clock again. 5:45 pm. *Fifteen more minutes*, she reminded herself. Why she felt the need to clock watch all afternoon, she didn't know. *Okay, she did know. She was ready for Ian to come to the café. There, she admitted it. He intrigued her.* She slid the last small clump of cheese down the grate and grabbed another block of sharp cheddar and began the routine again. She had owned the café for three years. It was the realization of a dream she had possessed since she was a little girl: a café on the edge of the city, bridging the gap between the suburbs and the hustle and bustle. She smiled thinking of several of her regular customers, an eclectic group of people, yet each person brought a smile to her face almost every single day.

She paused in her grating as she heard a knock on her back door. Smiling, she turned and saw Sara standing in the window. Unlocking the door, she let her friend inside. "I thought you finished up at five?" Kat asked.

"No, I had to do some prep work for a potential client meeting tomorrow. I am headed to Travis' now though; I'm going to stay over there tonight considering our house may not be safe."

"I think you would be fine since I am staying here." Kat looked at the clock again. *Five more minutes.*

"Travis told me Ian volunteered to stay here with you. Don't you think that's kind of..." Sara trailed off as Kat glanced up from her cheese grating.

"Kind of what?" She asked curiously.

"Selfish? On your end, I mean?"

"Selfish?" Stunned, Kat surveyed her friend. "Why would it be selfish?"

"Because he's worked a full day since 4:45 this morning responding to your first call of alarm, and then he's going to pull an all-nighter with you here and then turn around and work a full day tomorrow."

"I thought he was off tomorrow?" Kat asked.

"No, today was supposed to be their day off." Sara corrected, a slight edge to her voice.

"Oh. Well I am sure he would not have volunteered if he knew he couldn't handle it."

"Really? That's your response?" Sara shook her head in dismay. "He's risking his life for you, Kat. You are in danger. What do you not understand about that?"

"I understand fully." Kat countered. "I also know that I cannot let a little fear stop me from making a living. I have bills to pay. A business to run. A house to pay for. I cannot do those things if I am running away with my tail between my legs."

"All I am saying, is maybe you should think of others right now too. I mean, we are roommates. You being in danger puts me in danger. You being in danger puts Jeremiah in danger. Ian. Amy. Travis."

"And anyone else I come in contact with, I know." Kat finished.

"Then why won't you say anything?" Sara asked.

"About what?!" Finally, Kat tossed the block of cheese onto the counter and placed her hands on her hips. "I don't know anything. I don't know why these attacks are happening, Sara. All I know is that they did not start happening until you ratted out whomever was meeting in our alleyway. The only reason you are not the target is because you never dated Marshall. They assumed it was me, for that very reason. Otherwise, you could be the one in my position. I would think you would cut me some slack considering I'm in this mess because of you."

"Because of me?!" Sara's voice rose and slightly cracked as she crossed her arms and her eyes narrowed. "I reported a crime."

"No. You told your overprotective boyfriend that you were scared," Kat pointed out and received the smoldering glare she knew was coming.

"Would you rather have drug runners meeting in your alleyway? By all means Kat, just put a vacancy sign up and let them set up shop, why don't you?" Sara's voice rose as she began pacing back and forth.

"That's not what I'm saying."

"Right. Well, blame me for all I care." Sara continued. "I want to feel safe while I am at work, and if that means running to my boyfriend to ask for his help then so be it. I thought I was doing the right thing. I thought I was being a good friend by also protecting you. But whatever." She grabbed her purse from the counter and shouldered it as she reached inside for her keys. "You just stay here tonight and put yourself at risk. Put Ian at risk. He's too new to know better any way."

"New? He's been a detective for six years!" Kat challenged.

"Not new to the job, Kat. New to knowing you."

"What's that supposed to mean? That he doesn't know better?"

"Yes, that is exactly what it means. Sometimes you just push and push and push until you get what you want, without thinking of others in the process. People could get hurt this time, Kat. Just remember that while you-"

Her words were cut off by a knock on the kitchen door. Kat jolted and noticed Sara's wide eyes. "Why is someone out there? Did you not lock up?"

"I thought I did." Kat reached behind a cabinet and produced a baseball bat. Sara shuddered as she ducked behind a table as Kat nudged the kitchen door open. She jumped back with a fierce swinging position as Ian held up both his hands in surprise. "Whoa now, I realize I'm a few minutes late, but take it easy."

"How did you get inside?" Kat asked.

"The front door was unlocked." He motioned over his shoulder. "I locked it behind me. You really shouldn't leave it unlocked while you are alone."

"I didn't." Kat put the baseball bat down and turned as Sara appeared again.

"Hello, Sara," Ian greeted. "I'm sorry to have scared you both."

"No apology necessary, Ian. You further proved a point I was trying to make to Kat."

"No, he didn't."

"Um, yes, he did." Sara motioned towards him as Ian stood between the two women and watched them throw flames with their eyes at one another.

"Jeremiah left through the front entrance today. He must have forgotten to lock up behind him," Kat stated.

"Putting you at risk. Because you are not safe," Sara countered.

"Sara, the longer you stand here and argue with me, the more you are at risk. I thought that was what you were trying to avoid." Kat motioned towards the back door and Sara glowered at her.

"You're right. How stupid of me," she mocked, turning to leave. "Hopefully I will see you tomorrow." She stepped out of the café and hurried to her car, Kat leaning to make sure Sara made it there safely.

"She is just worried for you."

"And herself." Kat mumbled. "Sorry, I shouldn't have said that. I'm struggling with being slightly upset at her for starting this mess, when in reality it is my ties to Marshall that has put me here."

"Either way, it's not a fair situation. So, do you know what I recommend?" Ian walked over to the sink and washed his hands.

"What's that?" Kat asked, her mood already lightening at his presence.

"I suggest you show me the ropes and teach me your ways, Kat Riesling. Because I am here to help you. So put me to work." He flashed a devastating smile that had Kat's heart racing a bit faster as she returned it.

"I like your style, O'Dell. I like your style."

∞

Two hours later, Kat found herself throwing her head back and releasing a deep laugh as Ian tossed dough into the air and it landed on the floor. "I think you should keep those moves to a minimum." Kat grabbed the dough and tossed it into the trash. "This is not a pizzeria."

"Have you ever thought about making pizzas?" he asked curiously, as he grabbed another ball of dough and began rolling it out the way she had demonstrated to him earlier.

"I have, but I don't think it would be fair to Tony up the street. That's sort of his thing." She handed him a bowl of chopped strawberries as she popped one into her mouth in the process. She studied his work and nodded. "Not bad, O'Dell." She walked back to the other end of the long table where she worked faithfully slicing different fruits.

"Do you normally do all this prep work yourself?"

She looked up and grinned. "Yep. It's sort of my favorite part. I love preparing food for people. Jeremiah is the friendly face that loves to talk with people and interact. I'm more the behind-the-scenes girl."

"Ah, Jeremiah." Ian paused, watching as she sliced and pitted several peaches with quick efficiency. "How long have you known him?"

She quirked a suspicious eyebrow and smirked. "Are you asking for professional reasons or for friendly conversation?"

"Can it be both?" he asked.

She waited a moment as they studied one another. "I'll let you get by with it this once." She waved him back to his work as she continued. "I've known Jeremiah for about three years. I met him not long after I opened the café."

"How'd you two meet?" He heard her sigh and knew his line of questions would soon be unanswered.

"It's sort of a long story. I'll just say I met him here at the café."

"Was he your best customer?"

"Not exactly. More like my worst." She chuckled to herself as she moved towards his end of the table and began spooning fruit inside the dough and rolling them to make crescents. She placed them on a baking sheet and slid the full sheet onto a rolling rack for the cooler. She then helped him finish his and began rolling the rack to the giant freezer, propping the door open with a cat shaped door stop. She grabbed several packages of dough she had already prepared, nudged the door stop out of the way, and then placed the dough on the table.

"What are we making now?"

"Cookies." She smiled as he walked towards her to help. As he stood next to her, his shoulder brushed hers and she took a moment to bask in the light scent of his cologne that wafted through the air. She took a sharp knife and sliced several pieces of dough and placed them on a cookie sheet. "Think you can handle this?" He nodded, reaching for the knife, his fingers brushing hers. She quickly pulled

Chicago's Best

her hand away and walked towards her end of the table to begin work on something else.

He watched as she liberally began spreading dressing on slices of ciabatta bread for sandwiches. "Do these need to go inside the fridge?" He asked, as he motioned to the completed trays before him.

"Wow, you're fast." She smiled appreciatively. "We are actually going to go ahead and bake those." She grabbed a few trays and stuffed them inside the oven and grabbed several more and did the same.

"Does this job involve sampling?"

She laughed. "Maybe. If you're good."

He held up his hand as if taking an oath. "On my honor."

"All right. Then for now, while those are baking, you can help me make these sandwiches." She handed him a knife and a bowl of spread. "Both sides, liberally."

"Got it." He watched her complete one before beginning, an act she appreciated as she continued. "These going in the box lunches you're preparing for tomorrow?"

"Yep." She pointed to a stack of bright green cardboard.

"We have to fold all of those, don't we?" he asked, slight dread in his voice.

"Yep." She replied cheerfully. As she passed by him, she patted him on the shoulder. "But don't worry, when we are delirious at 2 am, it goes by a lot faster."

"I will admit to needing some coffee soon. It has been quite a long day."

"Of course. I should have had some waiting for you. I'll put some on." She bustled over to a small cabinet and began the work of filling the coffee grounds into the machine and situating the carafe. Soon, the sounds and smells of brewing filled the kitchen. He inhaled deeply. "Just the smell has brought me to life."

Laughing, she fetched two mugs and watched as he continued working. "I want to thank you, again, for coming to keep an eye on me and help."

He turned to briefly glance over his shoulder. "No problem. I figured you would probably be up here regardless of our warnings, so might as well make sure you're safe."

"Yeah." Her voice quieted as she thought back to Sara's words. "I do not mean it to be selfish, if that's how it comes across. It's just..." She trailed off as he turned to watch her. "Well, this is my livelihood. I can't really afford to lose business."

"I understand. I do not think it selfish, and if I may be so bold as to say so, I think Sara was completely out of line earlier."

"You heard all of that?" Kat's face flushed as he nodded.

He held up a hand and took a step towards her. "Please, I was not trying to eavesdrop, and please do not be embarrassed. I thought your points were valid. Yes, she did the right thing in reporting the suspicious activity, but her blaming you for putting others at risk is completely out of line."

"She is sort of right, though." Kat admitted. "I mean, you would not be here if I wasn't insisting on doing all this." She waved her hand around the kitchen.

"It would be here or at your house, Kat."

"I'm sorry?"

"What I mean is, I would either be here with you or staking out your house all night to make sure no one harmed you. And by the smell that's coming out of that oven over there, I am glad you chose the café this time around. I benefit in a most delicious way." He smiled, and she felt the sudden urge to hug him for saying such kind words. But she refrained as she walked towards the oven and slipped the trays of cookies onto cooling racks. "You're just in luck then, because these babies are finished. Let me pour you a cup of coffee and then we can take a break, eat some dinner, have a cookie, and then get back at it." She walked over to a separate toaster oven and pulled out two plates. "I've had this going for a while to keep warm. I hope you like chicken pot pie."

"Seriously? What man doesn't?" He winked as he accepted his plate and sat on one of the stools at the worktable. She sat opposite him and sighed as she rolled her shoulders. "I need a glass of wine." She started to move and he held up his hand. "I'll get it. Where's it at?"

She pointed to a closet and he opened the door to find racks full of bottles. "Which one?"

"Any one."

He pulled a Sauvignon Blanc and came back to the table. "Glasses?"

She pointed to a set of shelves above the plate shelves. He retrieved two glasses. "Corkscrew?"

Smiling, she pointed to a utensil holder on the counter. He grabbed it and set about opening the bottle. His cell phone rang and he reached into his pocket and swiped the screen. Holding the phone against his shoulder and mouth he answered, "O'Dell." He finished opening the bottle and let it breathe a moment as he listened. "All is quiet, Starr... No, nothing... I will. Later." He hung up and stuffed his phone back into his pocket.

"Travis checking up on me?" she asked.

Nodding, he slid a glass in front of her as he took his seat again. "He seems to care for you a great deal."

"He better," she teased. "He's dating my best friend."

A light scratch sounded on the back door and had Ian bolting to his feet and waving Kat down. She held up her hands. "Whoa, hold on a second. I know that sound. It's not a criminal, Detective. It's just Kissa wanting her nightly grub." She walked towards a closet and grabbed a bag of cat food. He briskly walked over and stood between her and the door. He halted her protest with his fingers on her lips, a mistake he realized as soon as his eyes found hers. He dropped his hand. "I should at least check to make sure first." He turned before Kat could see the affect she had on him. He unlocked the door and slowly eased it open. Three hungry cats sat eagerly on the stoop in front of him with pitiful meows as they waited. Kat grinned at them and clicked her tongue as she shook the bag and the cats paced joyfully waiting her to pour some out for them. "Told you." She dumped a generous amount on the concrete and gave them all a long petting before closing the door and locking it again. She then headed to the sink and washed her hands.

She sat back down and waited for him to join her. He shook his head while he smiled.

"What?"

"You and your cats." He laughed, the sound deep and pleasing as his green eyes lit up.

"I can't help it. I found them when they were kittens. I couldn't let them die. Believe it or not I do have a soft side every now and then." She took a sip of her wine and then a bite of her meal.

"I believe it. It takes a lot of love to feed people and you put a lot of care and passion into your work. It is evident." He complimented.

"Wow." Her brows rose. "You would be the first person, besides Jeremiah, to ever think that I'm sure."

"I doubt it."

"Um, you did hear Sara earlier, right?"

"She is just scared. She has a right to be, but she is just worried and scared. Her words stemmed from that, not from her heart. Otherwise, I do not see how you two have been friends as long as you have." He explained. "You also have a strong head about you. Sara does not. It is not something she can understand."

"Wow." Kat said again, pleased with his explanation but also a little surprised. "You don't think much of Sara, do you?"

He choked back on the sip of his wine and beat his chest. "No, that's not how I meant for that to sound. She seems pleasant enough and has a pretty face. She seems to care for Travis and vice versa. I just meant that she is different than you and cannot understand you sometimes because of those differences."

"You've known us a couple of days and you seem to have us figured out pretty well." Kat sipped on her wine as she studied him.

"I've had my share of experience in studying people."

"Has anyone studied you?" she asked with a mischievous glint in her eye.

"I'm a tough one to figure out." He grinned as he finished off his plate and took it to the sink to wash.

"Oh really? I doubt that. Men are pretty easy to figure out."

"Is that so? Think you have me figured already?"

"No. I'm working on it."

"Ah, I see. Well let me know your findings when you do."

"I will." Her cheeks began to hurt from all the smiling she had been doing since Ian arrived and she quietly pondered how long it had been since that happened.

"More?" He motioned to her wine glass and she nodded.

He topped off her glass and then waited for instruction. She grabbed a couple cookies off the cooling rack and handed him one as she took a bite of another and walked about the kitchen. His teeth sank into sugar and chocolate and he closed his eyes as he let the flavor melt inside his mouth. "Wow. These are incredible," he mumbled over a full mouth.

She grinned as she moved two large roasting pans to the worktable. "Secret recipe."

"Is the secret love?"

She laughed. "Um, no. Why?"

"That is just what my mother always says."

"Aw. Look at the big bad detective talking about love and his momma." She noted the blush to his neck as he took a sip of wine and shrugged. "It's sweet." She continued. "Hopefully one day my kids will speak the same way about me."

"You have kids? I didn't notice them the other day at your house?" His brow rose slightly.

"No. No kids. I meant in the future. You know, if I can ever find someone who can stand me enough to marry me and have kids." She swirled her hand around as she spoke, the other uncapping the roasting pans. Steam lifted into the air, and he noted the tendrils around her face slowly begin to curl. "I imagine you will have a houseful one day." He meant it as a compliment and her awkwardness as she picked out the utensils they would need told him it did not go unnoticed. Though she played his comment off, she took a long sip of wine as she continued her work. "This is steak. We are going to make cheese steak sandwiches. You just take a good amount like this." She showed him how to apply the meat and cheese slices before wrapping it up in foil. She then placed the sandwich on a baking tray. "We wrap every single one and tomorrow they will go into the oven and bake so they get all melty and delicious."

"I feel I should be writing some of this down." He patted his pockets as if searching for a pen and she rolled her eyes.

"It's a sandwich, O'Dell, it's not that complicated."

He winked at her as he began working on the sandwiches before him and they continued in easy conversation. Kat glanced up at the clock, the hand slowly ticking towards midnight. They had accomplished quite a bit and she felt grateful for Ian's help, but she was slowing down. Sheer exhaustion had made her movements sluggish, and she wondered how he seemed to keep up his stamina. She sat on the stool and paused for a moment.

"You okay?" He asked, his brow furrowed as he set aside his work.

"Yes. Just all of a sudden hit a wall. I'm tired." A lazy smile filtered over her face due in part to the second bottle of wine they had opened and also in part to her being tired.

"Take a breather. I can finish these." He picked up the next sandwich and began layering it as she showed him.

"I'm sure you are tired too."

He shrugged his shoulders. "I'm sort of used to the crazy hours and long stretches of no sleep. You going to make it until five?"

"I'm not sure. I'm going to try."

"You could always go home and get a few hours shut eye and then come back."

"No. I need to finish all this. I think it is time I just work on muffin batter. Something easy that I don't really have to think about for a while." She slid off the stool and listlessly made her way around the kitchen.

Sympathy had him wrapping his last sandwich, moving the tray to the refrigerator and walking towards her. He placed his hands on her shoulders and she immediately tensed. "Let me." He lightly nudged her aside. "You pull up a stool and tell me what needs to be done, and I will do it. You need to rest a few minutes."

"I can do it." She challenged, but even to her ears it sounded half-hearted. He shook his head and pointed at the stool he pulled over. "Sit. Now what's next?"

She walked him through several batters and before she knew it the first batch of muffins were coming out of the oven and he was prepping the next round. "I think you should quit your job at the station and come work for me."

He tossed her a smile before wiping his hands on a towel and slinging it over his shoulder. The movement was oddly appealing. "What next?" She pointed to the refrigerator. "There should be a blue crate with more cookie dough wrapped in logs. We need to slice up and bake more of those."

"Wow, there are all kinds in here. You've been holding out on me."

She went to stand and he tisked before pointing back at the stool. "I've got this. Same as we did the others?"

"Yes." She smiled in thanks as she leaned her head on her hands and watched him. "What do you think I should do?" she asked.

He looked down at her and continued slicing and placing cookies onto baking sheets. "What do you mean?"

"About all this trouble that's going on. What should I do about it? About Marshall?"

"I don't really think there is much you can do at this point. Unfortunately, it is a waiting game. We are trying to figure out Marshall's stake in all of this and the connection that he may have. We think you are being attacked based on your past relationship with him."

"But I don't understand why? That was almost a year ago."

"Maybe these guys do not know that."

She sighed heavily as she rested her head on her hands. He knew it was only a matter of time before she fell asleep. "I really thought I was done with

Marshall." Her words were muffled against her hands, and defeat sank her shoulders.

"You will be. I will help make that happen."

She looked up and met his gaze. "Thanks."

"You're welcome." He continued slicing the dough and pretty soon heard her even breathing. Watching her, he quietly continued his work, hoping that the woman before him could catch some rest amidst the chaos that had suddenly taken over her life, and he prayed he could keep her safe until they figured out who was after her and why.

«CHAPTER FOUR»

THE DOORKNOB SHIFTED AND Ian dropped the knife from his hand and quickly snatched the gun hidden in his ankle holster aiming it at the back door to the café. He stealthily made his way to the wall next to the door and waited with his back against the wall to see who entered. The doorknob wiggled again and then slowly the door began to open. A man's shoe stepped over the threshold and Ian had him by the collar and slammed against the wall with a gun to his temple before the man could mutter a sound.

"Whoa, man!" Jeremiah's gray eyes widened in shock. Ian did not release his hold.

"What are you doing here?" His voice was low, barely audible as he tried to keep from waking Kat.

"Um, I work here." Jeremiah replied, annoyance in his gaze as he pointed to the gun. "You going to lower that?"

Ian slowly released Jeremiah's shirt and slid his gun back into his holster. "What are you doing here right now?" Ian asked.

"I always get here at this time." Jeremiah pointed to the clock before confidently walking over to the small closet and retrieving the cat food bag. He opened the door and shook the bag twice before the three dumpster cats came calling. He poured a generous amount of food on the stoop before closing the door and putting the bag away.

Ian glanced at his watch. The time had flown and it was now five in the morning. The night had gone by fast, and he looked up to see Kat still sleeping with her head on her hands.

Ian walked towards the oven and grabbed a towel to retrieve the trays of cookies that were finished baking. He placed them on the cooling racks and then inserted more trays. Jeremiah watched with a small smirk on his face.

"Do you normally come to the café without letting Kat know first?" Ian asked, his question direct and

Jeremiah tried not to interpret the tone as suspicion.

"Well, normally I arrive when my shift is to begin, which is now, by the way. But when she pulls an all-nighter, I text before coming down so I don't scare her. I texted her phone, but obviously she didn't get it." He motioned to the sleeping form of Kat.

"She needed rest," Ian defended.

Jeremiah held up his hands in peace. "Hey, I know that is a fact. I'm not complaining to find her asleep. In fact, I'm quite impressed you got her to sleep."

"I didn't have anything to do with it."

Jeremiah sighed at Ian's harsh tone. "Dude, seriously, what is with the attitude? I am friends with Kat. Travis and Sara, too, if you must know. When are you going to trust me?"

"When you are honest with me," Ian replied.

"Okay, ask me whatever then. I've got nothing to hide." Jeremiah began working on the coffee machines adding multiple brews to multiple pots.

"You have a criminal record," Ian stated.

"And?" Jeremiah asked. "Lots of people have criminal records."

"Care to explain yours?"

"I had a rough past. I stole some things. They were all misdemeanors, nothing big. I served out my sentences or community service."

"What did you steal?" Ian pressed.

"Shouldn't the police reports show that?"

"I didn't look. I just looked at what you were charged for."

"I see. So naturally you jump to the conclusion that because I stole a few things, I *must* be linked to the largest drug ring in Chicago."

Ian shrugged. "I've seen it before. The fact that you are within Kat's inner circle makes you an asset."

Blowing a breath of frustration, Jeremiah shook his head. "You must have some serious trust issues, man."

"Doesn't matter what I have." Ian challenged. "Now answer the question. What did you steal?"

"Mainly food." Jeremiah replied. "Or this one time I squatted at a hotel room and gave them a bogus credit card number and didn't pay for the room. I really just needed a bed for the night. Stole some clothes once."

"Why?"

"I had a rough go for a while. It's what I did to get by."

"And why the turnaround? What made you decide to work for Kat?"

"She didn't really give me much of a choice." Jeremiah chuckled at his own words and as he looked adoringly at Kat.

"How's that?" Ian watched as Jeremiah shifted from coffee pots to display trays, stacking muffins and pastries that Ian and Kat had baked in order to move them to the front glass cases at the counter.

"Have you noticed we give Kat a hard time about her cats?" Jeremiah asked.

Ian nodded and waved for him to continue, hoping he would receive more information before Kat woke up and heard him questioning her friend.

"We tease her, because they are strays. We joke that she has a soft spot for strays, because she takes them in. I was somewhat of a stray. Kat found me in her alleyway digging for scraps one evening. She brought me inside. Made me wash up, fed me, and then made me sweep and mop the entire café to earn the meal she had just given me. Then she told me to sleep in the office on the cot she has there. It was the first night of decent sleep I had had in months. When I awoke, there was a change of clothes and an apron. She put me to work immediately."

Ian's brows rose in surprise at his story. "And you have worked here faithfully ever since?"

"I owe her my life. I would do anything for her. Plus, I love working here. She let me get a few months under my belt and when I could afford to, I rented out the loft from her upstairs. I'm back on my feet because of her. So yeah, I've worked here for the last three years and I will continue to work here. I was her first stray."

Ian studied Kat and he felt a small part of him long to know that tender side of her. The soft spot she rarely showed to others.

Jeremiah stepped by him and grabbed a clean washcloth. "She's a great catch, man."

"Oh, I didn't realize you two were involved on a more personal level." Ian immediately shook away his previous line of thinking.

Jeremiah laughed. "We are not involved. I'm just telling you that she is a great catch if you are interested. It will take her a while to let her guard down, thanks to Marshall and the drama he brought to her life. But I promise you, man, she is worth the wait and the work."

"My relationship with Ms. Riesling is strictly professional." Ian reminded Jeremiah and inwardly himself.

Jeremiah grinned as if he did not believe him before turning to tap Kat on the shoulder. "Wake up, sleepy head."

Kat jolted and immediately grabbed Jeremiah's hand and swung it over her head and wrenched it behind his back, and forced her other arm into the middle of his back as she slammed him face first into the worktable and held him there.

"Kat! Kat! Kat! It's me!" He grimaced as she quickly released him.

"Jer! I'm so sorry! I was just... you should know better than to sneak up on me!" She hugged him briefly before rubbing his shoulder. "You okay?"

"I'm fine." He chuckled as he squeezed her hand.

Ian stood to the side and watched, impressed that Kat had self-defense skills. Intrigued that her first instinct from being awakened was to fight, he wondered what event had happened to her to make that her first response.

She caught his eye and then flushed. "I promise I usually don't attack people."

He held up his hands. "I didn't say a word."

"You had that look."

"What look?" Amused, he waited for her to answer.

"You're trying to read me and figure out why I reacted the way I did."

"It's my job."

"Well stop working for a minute." She pointed at him as her gaze surveyed the green boxes lined up on the back counter, all folded with napkins, a cookie, and a bag of chips inside. "You did all this?" She asked, her hand slowly lowering back to her side.

He nodded. "If it's wrong, I apologize. I was just trying to help. I looked at your list." He pointed to the paper she had been following throughout the night before continuing. "You had the lunch boxes listed out with what you wished to include in each one. I have everything but the sandwiches in there. I figured you would probably be baking those later so they were warm. Everything else, I just sort of consolidated onto trays once it was finished. I wasn't sure where you put the cookies or muffins."

"You finished baking all the cookies and muffins?"

"Yes. Is that not what you needed?"

"No, that is exactly what I needed done. But why? Why didn't you wake me up?" She asked, rubbing a hand over her face as she attempted to rub away the night's sleep.

"You needed rest."

"Says the guy who is about to go pull another work shift." Kat walked towards him and stood a few inches away from him. She looked up at him and noticed the fatigue around his eyes, but his gaze remained sharp. She slid her arms around his waist and gave him a tight hug before pulling away and walking back towards the worktable. "Thank you." Her words were quiet as if she was unsure how to accept the help.

Ian, still thinking about having her arms around him, shook his head. "You're welcome."

Jeremiah's gaze fluttered back and forth between the two. Ian caught the sly smile on his face and then cleared his throat. "Speaking of which, I should head over to the station. My shift starts at six." He slipped off the borrowed apron and hung it on the hook by the door.

Kat tried to hide her disappointment. Ian caught her eye and then motioned towards the front entrance. "You will have an unmarked car outside all day. But if you are unsure about anything, call me, okay?"

Katharine E. Hamilton

She nodded.

He handed her a card. "My cell number is on the back. I mean it, Kat, please call if you sense any trouble."

A soft smile spread over her face as she studied him. "You're an oddity, O'Dell."

"How's that?"

"There are only a few good men in this world. One is my dad. Two is Travis. Three is Jeremiah. It takes a lot to rank up there with those men in my life, but you are slowly nudging your way up onto the list. Thank you, again. For all your help." She rubbed a hand on his bicep before sliding it down and squeezing his hand. "I appreciate it." She turned and walked towards her workstation. "Before you go, let me load you up with a box of goodies for the station and a fresh coffee."

Ian hesitated and pulled out his cell phone. Travis had texted him to check how the night went. He quickly responded and then glanced up as Kat walked back towards him with a large green box and two cups of coffee on top. "That one is for Travis." She pointed to the cup on the right. "This one is yours."

"What's the difference?" He heard Jeremiah laugh.

Kat smirked. "Travis drinks his coffee like a girl."

Katharine E. Hamilton

Ian laughed. "Oh really? There are such things as girl coffees and boy coffees?"

She shrugged. "Though not a politically correct statement, yes. Yes, there is. Lots of cream. Lots of sugar, and a little whipped topping with caramel sauce. I just hide it in a regular cup so as not to infringe upon his masculinity."

"You realize I will now give him a hard time?"

"That was my goal." She winked while opening the back door for him to exit.

He turned. "Remember, anything out of the ordinary, call me."

Nodding, she stepped forward and lightly kissed his cheek. "I will. Have a good day, Ian." She watched as he walked towards the end of the alleyway.

"You're checking him out, aren't you?" Jeremiah asked.

"You know it." Kat laughed as she shut the door and did not hide the smile on her face as she and Jeremiah began preparations for the morning rush.

∞

"Carnations?" Kat grimaced as she slid into the overly fluffed pink chair inside Sara's flower shop and watched her friend assemble an arrangement.

"Worse," Sara stated and peeked around the blooms. "Purple carnations."

"Yikes. Who's the lucky girl? Or should I say unlucky?" Kat flipped through a magazine half-heartedly as Sara chuckled.

"Please do not tell me Jeremiah is having you whip up something for a 'friend.' He should know better than carnations."

Laughing, Sara shook her head. "No. Although he did ask me to create something for a girl named Angela."

"Oh really?"

"Don't press him about it though. I think he's genuinely interested with this one."

"Don't you say that about all of them?" Kat asked dryly.

"Hey, it's business for me." Sara winked as she cut the finishing touches off a splice of ribbon. "Done." She placed the card into the plastic holder and spun the bouquet around for Kat's approval.

"Very nice. You're so good you can even make carnations look lovely."

"Good. Because they're for you."

Kat choked back her next retort with wide eyes. "What?"

"They're for you." Sara repeated. "I was asked to deliver them to you, but since you're here you can just take them with you."

"Who is sending me flowers?" Kat hopped up from the chair and snagged the card. "A secret admirer. Seriously?" She slapped the card back on the counter and turned to walk back to the chair. "Wait." She paused and turned, a small smile to her lips. "Who sent them, Sara?"

"I don't know." Sara wiped down her counter top.

"Tell me. You know you are terrible at keeping secrets." Kat's eyes twinkled as she clapped her hands. "Tell me. Was it Ian?"

Sara paused in her cleaning. "Are you wanting it to be?" Interest in her voice, Sara's mouth dropped open in shock. "You *like* him." She pointed a finger at Kat and Kat immediately swatted it away.

"No. I mean... we had fun last night. I was just curious if he sent them."

"Right." Sara laughed in disbelief. "You like him."

"Just tell me who they're from." Kat pushed.

"I don't know. Literally. There was a stack of cash and a note telling me what they wanted and who to send them to, and the card was already filled out."

"And you don't have cameras to see who came in here to drop it off." Kat finished in frustration.

"It's a mystery, even to me." She grinned. "But I find it extremely interesting you think they would be from Ian, *or* that you would even want them to be."

Kat shook her head, but a small blush stained her cheeks. "No. I was just..." She rolled her eyes at Sara's pleased expression. "We had fun and there was-"

"There was?" Sara prodded.

"Chemistry." Kat finished but turned to leave.

"Wait!" Sara laughed, grabbing the bouquet. "Better take these just in case they are from him. He should see you with them."

Kat accepted the vase. "What do I do if they are?"

"Then you enjoy them." Sara patted her on the shoulder as if she were a simpleton.

"But they're carnations." Kat stated.

Groaning in frustration, Sara grabbed Kat's shoulders and nudged her out the door. "Enjoy them any way. He doesn't know what you like yet. Maybe drop some hints or something."

"No, because it's not like I want him to send me flowers."

"Whatever." Sara shook her head in dismay. "Just go home and get some rest."

Kat looked over her shoulder at her friend one more time before walking to her car to head to the cottage for some shuteye. *What would she do if the flowers were from Ian? How did she feel about that?* Her heartbeat picked up its pace as she thought about his kind eyes and warm smile. Shaking her head at the silly notion, she turned the key and set out towards home.

«CHAPTER FIVE»

IAN CAUGHT THE PEN that was headed towards his face as Travis walked back into the room. "Wake up."

"I am awake," Ian grumbled as he clicked through a current case file. "Still nothing out of the ordinary on the thugs we booked the other night. No connections to Thompson."

"Did you think it would be that easy?" Travis asked.

"No. I just hoped for somewhat of a break."

Travis sighed as he sat and propped his feet up on his desk. He tossed a stress ball into the air and caught it. Looking at their case board he frowned. "We have to connect the dots somehow."

"No kidding." Ian turned to face the boards as well and began following their trail through evidence, arrests, and incidents. "It's just that nothing makes sense. Thompson clearly has ties with Biggs, we have established that based on his court record. What we cannot figure out is what illegal activities Thompson is involved in and why Biggs is after him."

"But are we even sure Biggs is after him?"

"*Or* why he is working with Biggs." Ian amended.

Travis pointed at him like he hit the nail on the head.

"You think Thompson is willingly working with Biggs?"

"Yep." Travis stated confidently.

"But why?"

"The obvious reason: money."

"Okay, so say that is true. Why the thugs outside Kat's café? Why the break in?"

"To scare her back into his arms?" Travis asked the room, though it only consisted of him and Ian.

"I don't understand. He loves her, therefore he terrorizes her so she will turn to him for support?"

"We've seen weirder circumstances." Travis pointed out.

"That just doesn't seem to fit. I feel like Biggs may know of Thompson's affections for her and is blackmailing him in some form or fashion."

"Could be, but I doubt it."

"Why not?"

"Look, I know Marshall Thompson," Travis began, "he is not one to be pushed around, especially over a woman. Besides, he and Kat had a messy break up, he would not want to bring attention back to their relationship."

"And again, why not?" Ian asked.

Travis sighed. "Look... Kat would kill me if she knew I told anyone."

Ian leaned forward as Travis' voice lowered. "Marshall was... abusive towards Kat."

Flashes of Kat's reaction to Jeremiah waking her at the café filtered through Ian's head as he listened. "He hit her?"

"More than that." Travis explained. "Yeah, he tossed her around a bit. Granted Kat gave as good as she got. She started taking self-defense classes and that helped. She just couldn't seem to escape him until she finally had the courage to press charges. But he was emotionally abusive as well. The man is a creep."

"If given the chance I would gladly pound him into the ground for raising a hand at her or any woman." Ian's voice grew hard.

"Speaking of Kat, though, and to brighten the mood," Travis' face split into a smile. "How was the all-nighter?"

"It was fine." Ian turned back to the files on his desk and avoided Travis' probing gaze.

"I see." Travis laughed. "Let me guess, you are madly in love with her, aren't you?"

Ian's head popped up and confusion laced his brow. "Why would you say that?"

"First, your head just popped up." He pointed out Ian's interest and Ian flushed at his obviousness. "Second, I know Kat. She's charming and a great catch."

"So it would seem." Ian stated. "You're the second person to tell me that."

Travis' brow rose in curiosity, but he did not ask questions. "I'm headed over to her place after clock out. Want to join me, Roomie?" He grinned.

"I need sleep." Ian mumbled as he logged out of his computer and rubbed a hand over his exhausted face.

"No need to go home and sleep on an empty stomach." Travis pointed out. "Come with me, grab some grub, then go home to sleep."

"I don't like going to places I have yet to be invited."

"I'm inviting you." Travis groaned.

"It's not your house to invite me to."

"Fine." Travis whipped out his cell phone and dialed. "Sara, hey, I'm bringing Ian with me to dinner... okay great, love you too... bye." He hung up and smiled. "There. Now you can come. Let's go." He grabbed his keys and twirled them around his finger. "I'll meet you there. Don't flake out on me."

Ian shook his head but couldn't contain the small grin that filtered over his face or the small satisfaction that seeped into his head at having the opportunity to visit with Kat again. Clicking off his computer screen, he grabbed his wallet and keys and followed Travis out of the station.

∞

Sara hopped to her feet as the front door to the cottage opened and Travis walked inside. He immediately swallowed her up into a big embrace and kissed her. When he pulled away, he glanced over to Kat sitting on the floor at the coffee table. "Coloring?"

"Yep. Coloring and wine. It's what we do." She pointed a colored pencil between herself and Sara.

"It's a stress relief," Sara explained. "We chat, drink, and color."

"Adorable." Travis remarked, accepting the kiss on the cheek from Sara as she walked back over to her spot and sat down. "Ian's going to join us for dinner. He's pulling into our driveway as we speak."

"Food is keeping warm in the oven." Kat motioned over her shoulder without glancing up. Travis mumbled under his breath at her lack of interest, but his eyes caught the large flower bouquet on the fireplace mantle. "Nice flowers."

Sara's smile widened as she looked up. "Kat has a secret admirer."

Travis' brows rose as he reached to open the front door for Ian before he could knock. "No kidding?" He nodded a greeting towards Ian as he stepped into the house.

"Hi Ian." Sara greeted cheerfully.

"Hello Sara. Kat, good to see you again."

Kat looked up and smiled politely as she took a sip of her wine.

"Are you... coloring?" He asked curiously.

She held up her work and waved a hand over her progress.

"That looks complicated." Ian stepped forward and eased onto the arm of the couch.

"It's actually relaxing. They are called 'Adult Coloring Books.' Yes, it's a thing. Here." She flipped through her book and tore a page out and handed it to him. "For when you need to decompress."

"I don't think O'Dell is going to sit and color, Kat." Travis laughed as he eased into a chair. "So, any thoughts as to who your secret admirer is?" He wriggled his eyebrows.

"No." Kat blushed before looking down at her paper.

"Do you know?" Travis asked Sara and she shook her head, retelling the story of the mysterious order and payment.

"Interesting." Travis playfully stroked his chin.

"I'm sorry, secret admirer? What did I miss?" Ian asked.

Travis pointed to the flower bouquet.

"I see." Ian noted Kat did not look up but instead took a large gulp of her wine. "Jeremiah?" He asked. "He seems to be a fan of yours."

Kat choked on her wine. "Um, no. Jeremiah has ordered flowers for another woman. Besides, he's like my annoying little brother."

"It's an interesting choice of flower." Ian commented, bringing Sara and Kat's gazes towards him.

"Why do you say that?" Sara prodded, sending Kat a hopeful glance.

Ian blanched. "Oh, I didn't mean to say that out loud. It's nothing."

"Oh, no you don't." Kat stood and slightly teetered before she walked over towards the bouquet. "Why an interesting choice in flower?"

"It's nothing."

"No. I want to know." She fisted her hands on her hips and waited.

Sighing, Ian ran a hand over his face. "I'm tired. I did not know what I was saying."

"Come on, O'Dell, spill it," Kat challenged.

"Well, it's just carnations are so…" he trailed off.

"So what?" Sara asked.

"Ugly." He cringed as if he were insulting the women.

Travis laughed. "Seriously dude? A flower is a flower."

Sara hit Travis hard in the shoulder and made him wince. "Sorry, babe." Apologetically he kissed Sara's hair.

"You think carnations are ugly?" Kat asked, squinting as if trying to read his thoughts.

"See, that look is why I did not want to tell you my thoughts. I've insulted your gift." He waved his hands as if he did not like all eyes upon him and stood as if he were about to leave.

"Whoa, whoa, whoa, slow down a minute detective." Kat called after him. "You didn't insult my gift at all. You confirmed my exact feelings. I cannot stand carnations. And worse, they are purple. Clearly my admirer knows nothing about me."

"Then why did you accept them?" Travis asked.

Kat exchanged a glance with Sara.

"Because Sara made them. I did not want them to go to waste."

Something did not ring true in her reply, but Ian could understand her not wanting to upset Sara as well.

"No thoughts on who the mystery guy is?" Travis continued.

"No. I think that is why it's called a secret." Kat rolled her eyes as she walked towards the kitchen. "I'm going to pull the food out. Come eat if you're hungry." She left the room and Travis cornered Sara with a stare.

"I honestly have no idea either. I thought maybe they were from you." She motioned towards Ian and his eyes widened in surprise.

"Me? Why would I send Kat flowers?"

Sara's cheeks reddened and she shrugged her shoulders. "I thought maybe last night at the café you two may have hit it off or something." Travis lightly brushed his hand over the back of her hair as she stood to walk towards the kitchen.

Ian did not respond as he heard a loud crash come from the kitchen. All three of them rushed towards the sound. Kat rubbed her shoulder as pasta littered the floor in a shattered bowl. Ian's gaze took in the broken glass around her bare feet, the broken sliding glass door, and

Katharine E. Hamilton

the pain etched on Kat's face. "What happened?" He stepped forward, glass crunching beneath his shoes. She ran a hand over her face and he noticed it shaking. He grabbed it and smoothed a thumb over her knuckles and waited until she met his gaze. He noted a hint of fear in her brown eyes. Travis had already hurried through the broken door to hunt down whoever had defaced the cottage and attacked Kat. "You okay?" Ian lifted a hand to her face and her eyes glistened as she nodded. "Let me help you out of here." He slid his hands around her waist and lifted her as if she weighed nothing, her arms sliding around his neck as he carried her over the glass and back into the living room. She sat on the couch and ran a hand through her hair.

"What happened?" Sara asked, folding a leg under herself and sitting next to Kat and rubbing a comforting hand on her back.

"I'm not really sure. I was getting the pasta out of the oven and walking towards the table and this rock or something flew through the door and nailed me in the shoulder. I didn't see anyone run off or anything. I just froze." She looked up at Ian and his face wore hard lines and fire leapt into his eyes. He looked up as Travis walked back inside. "Nothing." He reported. "Whoever it was is a fast runner or had some form of transportation waiting for them."

"We need to call the Chief-" Ian's sentence ended abruptly as he dropped to his knees in front of Kat. "Your shoulder is bleeding." He reached towards her as she glanced down at the growing red stain covering her shirt.

"That looks bad." Sara stood and motioned for Kat to stand as well. "We should take a look. You may need stitches."

"I'm fine." Kat shrugged away the fuss and walked down the hallway towards the bathroom.

"I don't like this." Travis said quietly. "Sara, pack a bag. You two are staying at our place tonight." Sara nodded without arguing. "I'll call the Chief. You go see if we need to take Kat to the hospital for stitches." He pointed to Ian and then whipped out his cell phone. Ian walked down the hall and tapped his knuckles on the door he saw Kat enter moments before. She cracked it open and peeked out. Relief flooded her gaze as she widened it to let him enter. She closed the door behind him. She held a hand towel on her shoulder.

"Let me take a look." Ian reached towards the towel and gently removed it. When he did, her wound began pouring blood once more. "This is deep, Kat. You need stitches."

"I know." She clenched her teeth as she pressed the towel against the wound.

"I'll take you. Grab some shoes and we'll head that way. Travis is on the phone with the Chief. I'm sure they will send a team to survey the scene. We have your statement already, so Travis can file that with the Chief as well."

Kat eased to a sitting position on the side of the bathtub.

"You alright?" Ian knelt in front of her and noticed her face had paled.

"Just a little lightheaded. Wine and blood. Not exactly the best combination."

"Ah, but there was coloring." He said cheerfully, receiving the small smile he had hoped for.

"Yes, there was that at least."

"Need me to carry you?"

"No." Kat inhaled deeply as she looked at him. "Sorry. What I mean is, no thank you. I think I can handle it myself. You've been more than helpful and kind. I'll have Sara take me so you and Travis can head home once the scene has been cleared."

"I am not letting you leave without an escort, Kat. You were just attacked. I'm going with you."

"Ian, you have not slept in almost 48 hours. You need rest."

"What I need is not important at the moment. You need stitches, and that is what we will be taking care of. I can sleep afterwards. Now, come on." He helped her to her feet and she struggled to maintain her footing, bracing herself against the wall.

"I just need a minute." She looked down at the blood-soaked towel and Ian saw the signs on her face before she dropped her grip on the towel and her body went limp. He caught her before she fell and swept her off her feet. He hurried through the living room and out the front door. Other officers had arrived and were working the scene as he carried her across the lawn. Travis spotted him and ran over.

"She passed out. I'm taking her to the hospital for stitches."

"Poor Kat's never been one to brave the sight of blood. Sara and I will catch up to you once I'm done here." Travis darted back across the street and Ian closed Kat into his truck and sped away to the hospital.

∞

"That should take care of it." The doctor snipped the end of the last suture. "Keep it dry for the next couple days."

Ian watched as Kat pulled the shoulder of her white shirt back up and over the bandage. The red stain contrasting against the white fabric like an apple in the snow. She looked up and caught his concerned green gaze. "I'm fine, O'Dell. Just a couple of stitches."

"Thirteen, to be exact." The doctor mumbled as he signed her chart and handed it to the nurse. "Not just a couple. Keep an eye on her."

"Of course. Thank you." Ian shook the doctor's hand and waited for him to exit. "Did he give you any medicine for pain?"

"Yes, but nothing more than a strong ibuprofen. I'll be fine though." She hopped off the exam table. "I'm assuming you are my ride home?"

"Yes, however, you will be staying at my place."

"Excuse me?" Her left brow arched.

"I mean," the color rose in his neck and flushed his face; "you and Sara will be staying at Travis' house across the street tonight. Your house is not safe at the moment."

"Can I at least go by my house to grab some clothes?"

"From what I gather, Sara packed you a bag already."

"I see." She tucked her hands into her front pant pockets. "Have they found what came through my door and hit me?"

"A cinder block."

She nodded. "It felt like that, that's for sure."

"We'll find who did this, Kat, I promise."

"Wow, that's a big promise to make."

"I'm good at what I do," Ian stated confidently, and with a slight edge to his voice.

Kat walked towards the door and lightly gripped his arm. "You need sleep, then you can go hunt down the bad guys, O'Dell. I trust that you and Travis will find who did this, but first you have to sleep."

"You're being too nice." He swiped a hand over his tired face. "This should never have happened while both Starr and I were there. We let our guard down and you got hurt."

"And it was no one's fault. None of us could have predicted something like that happening at my house. Now, take me to your house, Detective O'Dell." She winked playfully as she allowed Ian to escort her through the hospital and towards his truck in the parking garage. When they had reached their level in the garage, Ian clicked the button on his keys and his truck lights flickered as the doors unlocked. "Nice wheels," Kat complimented as they crossed towards the vehicle.

"Thanks. It's new." He led her with a hand on the small of her back. He felt a shiver rush up his spine and he froze, halting Kat as well.

"What? What is it?" she asked, looking up at him in concern.

His eyes flashed around the parking area. "I want you to sprint to my truck and lock the doors. Start the engine." He whispered quietly, placing his keys in her hand.

"W-what?" She asked with wide eyes. "What's wrong? Do you see someone?"

"Shhh, Kat. Please. Go. Now." As soon as the words left his mouth, an engine roared to life and a dark sedan headed straight towards them. "Run!" Ian shouted and shoved Kat towards his truck as he withdrew his sidearm and took aim. Windows lowered and several guns fired, bullets ricocheting throughout the lot. Kat ducked behind a car and hurriedly made her way towards Ian's truck. She slipped inside and locked the doors, turning the key in the ignition. She ducked low but kept a vigilant eye open for Ian. She couldn't see him.

"Come on, O'Dell. Come on," she whispered, her legs antsy and bouncing beneath her. "Come on."

115

Katharine E. Hamilton

The driver side door flew open and Kat slung her feet out from under her to kick the intruder. She was halfway extended before she saw Ian's face and he blocked her with his arm and lightly shoved them aside. "Sorry!" She swiped her hair out of her eyes as he peeled out of the parking space and raced after the sedan.

"Forget it. You were prepared, that's a good thing. Now buckle up." He grabbed his communication device from the dash and began spouting numbers and locations. "Hold on, Kat, and stay low. I'm not letting this car out of my sight."

She buckled her seat belt and slid down in her seat. "Are you okay? Were you hit?" she asked over the rush of her pulse and the sound of screeching tires.

"No." His grip on the steering wheel tightened as they took a turn too fast onto Lexington Avenue. "Keep your head down," he ordered, without glancing her direction. She watched him closely as he maneuvered through traffic and kept chase. His eyes were hard, his jaw tight, and his lips set in a firm line. She had never seen him in the line of duty, and though her life was currently at risk, she felt her heart do a flip. She heard sirens emerge around them and soon several flashing lights pursued the same vehicle. Ian's coms came to life as the chief's voice filtered over the line. "Stand down, O'Dell, officers are in pursuit." Ian kept following.

"Stand down!" The order came again, louder with a touch of fury. "So help me, O'Dell, I said stand down!" Ian growled in frustration as he took a sharp left turn onto another street as the remaining police cruisers sped by in pursuit of the sedan. He pounded on the steering wheel before composing himself. He turned to Kat and his face held restrained fury.

"What now?" she asked, the air knocked out of her lungs by the anger etched on his face. His features immediately softened at the sound of her voice and his shoulders relaxed. "I take you home." He turned the truck back onto the street and headed the opposite direction from the chase, silence hanging in the air as he brooded and Kat stared out the window.

∞

Travis opened the door as Ian hurried Kat up the front steps to the house. Ian shut it quickly and flipped the lock. "Any news?" he asked, looking to Travis as Kat walked towards Sara in the living room.

"Chief called, said they lost the sedan for about ten minutes. When they found it, it was deserted."

"Of course it was." Ian scoffed under his breath as he followed Travis' gaze out the front window.

"Same SUV has driven by three times in the last twenty minutes." He reported. "I've got Smithens tailing it one block over. He said it keeps circling by. He's running the plates now."

"What is going on?" Ian muttered as the SUV turned onto their street and slowly drove by. It pulled to the curb in front of the house and Travis and Ian shifted to the walls next to the window out of the line of sight.

"Kat! Sara!" Travis called. "Go to my bedroom and lock the door."

"Wha-"

"No questions. Just go." He cut them off and the fact the two men did not glance their direction had the two women hurrying down the hallway.

«CHAPTER SIX»

IAN WATCHED AS THE front passenger door opened and a large man exited the vehicle. He then reached for the back passenger door handle and opened the door. Marshall Thompson stepped out and straightened his suit coat.

"Thompson." Travis grumbled. "He's not to come in the house."

"Agreed." Ian mumbled back.

Travis reached for the front door and opened it carefully, not allowing Marshall's line of sight to penetrate into the remainder of the house.

Ian stood to the side of the door out of view and waited to hear what Marshall said.

"Travis." Marshall greeted with a warm smile. "Good to see you."

"Marshall. To what do I owe the pleasure?"

"I'm looking for Kat. I've tried calling her but she seems to be ignoring my calls. I need to speak with her."

"What makes you think she is at my house?"

Marshall smiled. "Really? Must we play these games?"

Travis stood firm and Marshall sighed. "Fine. When she comes out of your room or wherever she is, please tell her I need to speak to her, and that it is urgent."

"What is it in regards to?"

"That is for Kat and me to know."

"Then I'm sorry, I can't help you." Travis started to shut the door and Marshall's hand jutted out to stop it.

"I will not be played, Travis. She will return my call."

"Or what? You'll throw another cinder block at her? You'll have your thugs throw bricks through her café windows?" Travis baited.

"Cinder block?" His brows rose. "I know nothing about that."

"Right. I don't believe you."

Marshall shrugged. "Believe what you want, but I need Kat to contact me."

"The only way you will be communicating with Kat is through me, so I suggest you be more specific, or you forget about it."

Marshall stepped forward and Ian shifted. Travis cut his eyes towards him, holding him off.

"She has something of mine and I want... need it back." Marshall's voice was low.

"What does she have?"

"She knows." Marshall slipped his sunglasses back on and turned. "Good day, Travis."

Travis watched as Marshall slid back into the SUV and it sped away.

"I don't like the sound of that." Ian stepped away from the wall.

"He's lying." Travis walked towards the edge of the hallway. "Kat would never hide something from me if it meant protecting Marshall."

"Are you sure?" Ian asked.

Travis' brown eyes flashed with temper. "I'll ask her myself, if you don't believe me."

"Kat! Sara! Come on out!" Travis called.

Ian heard the bedroom door open and the women walked back into the living room. Kat walked towards Ian and stood next to him. He tried not to think about how that made him feel, but instead tried to keep his head.

"Kat, it was Marshall." Travis reported.

"What? What did he want?"

"Said you have something he needs."

Her brow furrowed. "Did he say what?"

"No. He said you would know." Travis crossed his arms.

Kat looked perplexed, but Ian shifted to look down at her. "Is there anything you can think of that you might know or possess of his?"

"No." She looked up at him in surprise. "I never stole anything from him. He never gave me anythi- wait." She held up her hand. "The only thing I have in my possession that Marshall ever gave me was a necklace."

"What kind of necklace?" Ian asked.

"A diamond one. Nothing extravagant, mind you, but that's the only thing I have. I don't see why it would be important, though."

"Where is this necklace now?"

"In a safe."

"Where at?"

"At my house."

Ian and Travis exchanged a look.

"Trav, I promise that is all I have. I don't know anything or have anything else." Her eyes pleaded for him to believe her.

"I believe you, Kat." A tender smile tilted his lips.

"What made you decide to keep the necklace?" Ian asked. "After you broke things off, why did you keep it?"

"I'm not exactly one of those women who receive a lot of gifts, especially something like a diamond necklace. And though it didn't work out with Marshall, I liked the necklace. I didn't see the point in selling it or giving it back to him. It was a gift and one I actually wanted to keep."

"Most women would rid themselves of any reminder of their abuser."

"Abuser?" she asked, narrowing her gaze at him and then flashing it towards Travis. "You told him?!"

"He's working the case, Kat. It's not exactly something I can keep secret."

She crossed her arms in frustration. "I'll have you know, Detective O'Dell," she barked. "I've never been given a piece of jewelry before until that necklace. So whomever it came from, I don't care. It was a nice piece that if I ever needed a little extra money, I could sell. It was security for me. Besides, why would Marshall be after a necklace?"

"Not sure. But I think we need to take a look at that necklace, and right now." Ian ignored her temper and walked towards the door. "Lead the way, Kat."

She shoved past him and ignored his closeness as he remained vigilant in watching the street as they crossed over to the cottage. She unlocked the door and stepped inside, disarming her alarm before heading further into the house and down the hall. She opened the far door on the left and walked into a spacious room in neutral tones. The only color that graced the room was a large pillow in the center of the bed. Cobalt blue. He eyed the large windows and watched as she crossed to a walk-in closet. She pulled a small blue box off the top of a shelf and opened it. "Is that it?" He asked.

She shook her head. "No. It's the key to the safe." She pulled out a small key and then walked towards the kitchen. She pulled a chair from the table and slid it towards the pantry. Climbing up, she stretched to retrieve a small lock box from the top shelf hidden behind several boxes of cereal.

"Interesting hiding spot." Ian commented, curious as to why she chose that location.

"I spend most of my time in the kitchen, whether here or at work. I hardly ever grab anything off the top shelf of the pantry. So I thought, who else would think to look up there?" She turned the key in the lock and pulled out a black felt jewelry box. She opened it and handed it to Ian. "Just a basic studded necklace."

He withheld his surprise when he looked down and noted the graduated diamond necklace. Clearly Kat did not know jewelry or she would not be hiding the expensive gift behind a box of cereal.

"Well? Do you think that is what he's after?" she asked.

"Most definitely." Ian closed the lid and slid it into his pocket.

"Hey!" Kat stepped forward and Ian shook his head. "It needs to go to the precinct. You do not need to keep something this valuable in your house, Kat."

"I'm sure it's only worth a couple thousand dollars. I doubt the diamonds are even decent cuts."

"Are you being serious right now?" Ian asked her sharply.

She took a step back and crossed her arms. "Yes. Why?"

"You are honestly telling me you have no idea how much this necklace is worth?"

"Why? Is it worth a lot? It isn't stolen is it?" Her eyes widened. "Did he steal it? Am I holding some old lady's necklace hostage?" She waved her hands over her face to cool down. She took quick deep breaths.

"Calm down, Kat."

"No. Clearly Marshall stole that necklace, and you don't want to tell me. Or..." She paused and turned stunned eyes on him. "Or you think I knew all along. You think I knew it was stolen."

His lack of response had her eyes watering. She shook her head and ran a hand through her hair. "I need to sit." She sat in a dining chair and looked up at him. "What happens now?"

"First, we keep this under wraps." Ian motioned for her to stand and began walking towards the front door. "Second, we figure out why Marshall may want the necklace. What does he need it for?" Ian reached into his pocket and held it out to her. Kat waved her hands. "I don't want it now. You hold onto it for me and do whatever you need to with it to figure out Marshall."

Ian slid it back into his pant pocket. "Deal." He offered a reassuring smile and she sighed. "We should head back over." He walked towards the front door and paused, surveying the street before stepping out onto the front porch. Kat allowed him to escort her back across the street. When they reached Travis' porch, she looked at him. "So what do you think the value of that necklace is? I noticed when you looked at it you could tell it was valuable."

"Let's just say I have a feeling it is worth a lot more than the couple thousand you gave it credit for." He grinned as they walked inside to an awaiting Travis and Sara.

∞

Kat tampered down her disappointment as the door to the café kitchen swung open and Jeremiah waltzed in with an empty tray. He paused in his replenishment of baked croissants and studied her. "Everything okay, Kat?"

She blinked a few times to clear her thoughts and looked up at him. "Yes. Sorry, I am just tired. Travis' guest bed sucks."

Jeremiah's lips twitched into a smile. "Are you sure that's all it is? You weren't daydreaming? About a certain, oh I don't know, detective?" He winked. Though she rolled her eyes, he could see the small flush that stained her cheeks.

"Not in the slightest. Just tired. Here, let me restock those. I'll bring them out in a few." She intercepted the tray from him and he dashed back out the door to man the counter. It felt good being back at the café and back into her routine. Though the armed officers stationed around the café carried the threat of disruption to that routine, she still felt somewhat at peace in the midst of her safe haven. The café was her baby, her safe place, and her dream come true. She loved every minute she spent within its walls, and now that her life seemed to be turning upside down, she inwardly prayed that the café would not be violated or destroyed in the process. She stacked the last of the croissants and walked through the swinging door. She paused as Ian leaned against the counter and nursed a coffee, his face glued to his phone screen. He looked up as she passed by him. "I didn't realize you were here," she greeted with a warm smile, a slight relief relaxing her shoulders.

"Just for a few minutes."

"Try an hour." Jeremiah called him out, as he slid a coffee across the counter to an awaiting customer.

"An hour?" Kat asked. "Why didn't you come back to the kitchen?"

Ian's mouth twitched into a small smile before he replaced it with what Kat could only deem his "detective look." "I am not here to guard you, Kat. I came to check on things and then I have to head back to the station."

"Oh." Disappointment laced her response and he reached up and tapped her chin with his knuckles.

"Glad to see you want me around." He grinned before finishing the last of his coffee.

"Here, let me at least refill that for you before you go." She grabbed his cup and set about mixing together the coffee of his choice. A choice, he realized he had never told her, yet she innately knew how he took his coffee. He grinned at that, knowing she was more perceptive than he gave her credit for. She slid it back to him.

"Thanks."

"You're welcome. Any news on... well, you know." She swiped a hand around her neck to indicate the necklace.

"A bit."

Chicago's Best

"And?"

"And I can't really discuss that with you at the moment."

"Why?" Her eyes narrowed in frustration before worry creased her face. "It was stolen, wasn't it?"

"No, no. Nothing like that. I'll fill you in more tonight when we get home."

The thought of home being shared with Ian made her skin hum. Yes, she and Sara had been camping out in Travis' extra guest room for the entire week since the cinder block incident, but the closeness to Ian only made Kat grow more and more attracted to him. She maintained her distance in hopes that her feelings would fade, but the handsome detective had a magnetic way of pulling her towards him.

He could tell his answer dissatisfied her. "I'll swing by after my shift ends and pick you up. Will you be able to leave around six?"

Hope lit her eyes and she smiled. "Yes, I can be ready by then."

He nodded. "Done then. I'll see you in a few hours. Take care and-"

"And if I need anything there are officers all around me, blah, blah, blah, blah, blah. I know." She smirked as he grabbed her chin in his hand

130
Katharine E. Hamilton

and lightly tugged her towards him. Her breath caught at the amused spark in his eyes.

"Keep it up, Riesling." His eyes darted swiftly to her lips and then back up, his hand releasing her face before he completed his thought of kissing her and ruining his leadership role on her case. He saw her inhale a sharp breath, matched by his own as he snatched his coffee and pocketed his phone. "Six o' clock." He repeated, before walking out the door.

Jeremiah whistled under his breath and had Kat turning around.

"Pretty sure there was some underlying fireworks there." He grinned and held up his hands in innocence. "I could be mistaken," he laughed, "but that was no ordinary departure."

She tossed a damp hand towel at him, Jeremiah catching it before it slapped him in the face. He continued to laugh at her retreating back as he watched Kat hide back inside the kitchen in embarrassment.

∞

Ian ran a hand over his face, his five o' clock shadow scratched against the palm of his hand as he rested his chin there. "So we basically have nothing." His frustrated growl had Travis swiveling to face him in his chair.

"No, we have a necklace, bought and paid for by Marshall Thompson. A necklace worth more than $250,000. I would say that is something." Travis pointed out. "The questions we have are: 1. Where did Thompson receive that kind of money, and 2. Why invest the money in a necklace he gave to Kat?"

"Insurance. It's a gimme." Ian replied.

"True. But why? Why not open a safe deposit box? An off-shore account?"

"He didn't want the money traceable." Ian shrugged. "It's a pretty common scheme."

"If the money came from Biggs, or was somehow cheated out of Biggs, and Marshall was trying to swindle him, then that would explain why Biggs' goons would be out on attack. But why Kat?"

"Maybe he found out about the necklace purchase. If he did, that would explain the attacks on Kat. He's trying to see if she has the necklace."

"That doesn't make sense though, especially since Marshall and Kat have been finished for a year or so. Why would he think she has it?"

"Maybe Thompson let it slip." Ian crumbled up a sheet of paper with his notes and tossed it towards the trash can without looking, the paper ball finding its home perfectly in the wastebasket.

"How do you do that?" Travis asked in amusement.

"What?" Ian turned around and noticed his successful launch and grinned. "Skill."

"Whatever." Travis laughed as he clapped his hands and pulled his feet from his desktop to the floor. He stood, grabbing his keys. "We need a break from this. I say we think on it tonight and tomorrow we will have fresh eyes. We can look everything over again. Maybe Kat can shed some light on when Marshall actually gave her the necklace. That would help narrow down the timeline more on when hostilities may have risen between him and Biggs."

"Good point." Ian stood and stretched his back. "You think Kat and Sara will cook again tonight?"

Travis grinned. "I hope so. I must say, despite the overly female scent in the house, the hot meals are not a bad deal."

"I don't mind the lingering smell of perfume." Ian admitted. "There's something quite..."

"Annoying?" Travis tried to finish for him.

"I was going with more of intoxicating."

"Right. Sara has this habit of spraying her perfume in the air and then walking through it. So now, my entire house smells like a woman's perfume because she never puts her perfume on in the same place."

"Perhaps it is her subtle way of telling you your house smells bad," Ian teased.

"Um, you live there too. Therefore, maybe you stink it up, not just me."

"I always smell nice."

Travis feigned a disgusted look. "Yeah, right. Although, I bet I could ask Kat and she would agree with you."

"What is that supposed to mean?" Ian looked genuinely perplexed and Travis decided it best to keep his comments to himself for the sake of not having Kat kill him. He knew Kat well enough to notice she was interested in Ian. He just wasn't quite sure yet if Ian felt the same.

"Nothing. Let's go. I'm starving."

"I'll be there in a bit. I'm going to swing by the café and pick up Kat."

"Oh really? Did she not drive today?"

"She rode with Smithens since he was part of her protection detail today."

"I'm sure Smithens could give her a ride home." Travis baited.

"Why? When I'm going to the same place?" Ian asked. "Anyways, we'll be there in a bit."

"Got it. I'm sure Sara has been home for a while and has a plan for dinner. Hopefully."

"If not, text me. Kat and I can figure something out on the way home."

"Deal." Travis shrugged into a jacket, the October evenings carrying more of a chill as of late. When the two men stepped out onto the front steps of the precinct, the clouds rumbled. "Better hurry." Travis warned. "Looks like we have a rough night ahead." A gust of wind barely carried his words as they raced to their vehicles. As Ian shut the door to his truck, the first fat drops of rain pounded against his windshield. He took a moment to look up at the brooding clouds and then started the engine to head towards Kat. The thought of ending the day with her made him eager to reach the café. He recognized his softness towards her, but he also knew nothing could come to fruition while the investigation took place or he would be removed from the case. Ian also hoped that once the investigation was finished that Kat would even want to make a place for him in her life. That was the real issue he pondered as pulled up against the curb and hopped out of his truck dodging rain pellets as he hurried inside.

The bell above the door jangled at his entry and Jeremiah glanced up with a friendly nod while he served other customers. Ian made his way towards the counter and waited for Jeremiah to finish before interrupting. Jeremiah's eyes flashed delight as he knocked on the kitchen door for Kat to step out. She emerged a few seconds later wiping her hands on a dishtowel. "What is it? I was just out here." Her annoyance was evident until she followed Jeremiah's gesture towards Ian. Her face lifted into a welcoming smile. "Oh, well it is about time, O'Dell. I was about to start a new project back there."

"I said six," he reiterated.

"And it's six-thirty," she added.

"Well, I had to drive over here." He was surprised that she would hassle him over the miniscule time difference.

"Right. You're right. I apologize. I didn't think of that. Well, give me one second to put this towel away and grab my purse and then I'll be finished."

"Take your time." He watched her turn back into the kitchen.

"She was worried about you." Jeremiah explained. "She's been clock watching for the last half hour."

"Why would she be worried about me?" Ian asked.

Jeremiah gave him a look of restrained annoyance. "Really man? Surely you can tell Kat is loyal to her friends. She freaks out if I'm late by two minutes. Now imagine a guy she is starting to care about as more than a friend is half an hour late."

"I think you have her attentions misconstrued," Ian pointed out. "She's probably nervous about the case and all that's happened."

"I don't know, O'Dell. I've caught her daydreaming a couple times today, and I don't think they had anything to do with the case." Jeremiah dried a coffee cup before stacking it next to the brewer.

Ian did not know what to say. He had just warned himself to keep his intentions and affections under wraps until the investigation came to a close, but what was he to do with this new information? Clearly, Jeremiah thought Kat had feelings for him. And though he wasn't fully certain, he had started to feel a shift in the way Kat treated him. The thought pleased him and made his heart pound a bit faster as he watched her step out of the kitchen wrapping a scarf around her neck.

"Jer, I've placed everything in the freezer for now. When you leave tonight, be sure to transfer it to the refrigerator."

"Got it."

She lightly kissed his cheek in thanks. "You're a good man, my friend."

"I know." He smiled as she rolled her eyes and turned towards Ian.

"Ready?"

Ian nodded. Kat paused as she saw the downpour outside the windows. "Wow. I didn't realize it was raining. I didn't bring an umbrella."

"You guys will have to make a run for it." Jeremiah waved his hand as he watched them walk to the door. Kat paused briefly before pushing outside and darting towards Ian's truck. She saw the flash of his lights as he unlocked the doors and as she reached for her door handle, she startled as a hand grabbed it first. Ian opened the door and she dove inside and watched as he ran around the front of his truck to hop into the driver's side. They were both soaked from the rain and he turned his heater up to compensate the wet and chilly weather.

"You didn't have to open my door for me in the rain." Kat unwrapped her soggy scarf as he pulled out onto the street.

"Habit."

She sighed as she felt the warmth from the heater seep through her damp clothes. "I'm not complaining, just feel bad you had to stand in the rain longer."

"It's nothing." He offered a quick smile as he went back to watching his mirrors. His intensity set alarm bells to ringing inside her head.

"What is it? Is someone following us?" She nervously asked while turning to peer out the back window.

"No. I'm just being watchful."

"Oh," she relaxed as she turned back to face the front. "You're awfully short today. Did you have a rough day?"

Ian knew he was trying to hold his feelings at arms length, especially since Jeremiah picked up on them, but he had not realized his attitude had taken a turn in the process. "Sorry, no. I just... just want to make sure we are being cautious."

"I understand." She seemed to accept his reasoning. "Did Travis say whether or not Sara was cooking tonight?"

"We were hoping you ladies had talked."

"Well that answers that. Sara is not going to lift a finger in the kitchen unless she absolutely has to, so her silence speaks louder than words. You okay with lasagna for tonight? I can whip that up pretty fast when we get home."

"Lasagna? Are you kidding me?" he asked curiously.

"Um... no." She looked at him in confusion.

"I love lasagna, but growing up that was always what we ate on special occasions because it took my mom a long time to make it. Does it not take long?"

She smiled at his recollection. "Sometimes it can. Depends on how she made it. I have a couple of recipes I use. One can take forever, but the other is for my quick fix. Which is the one we will be having tonight."

"Ah, I see."

"What type of special occasions did your mom make it for?" She noticed a soft smile that swept over his face as he thought about his mom and she found it endearing.

"Oh, it could be anything. Winning a baseball game. Making the honor roll. When I graduated from the police academy. When I was promoted." He waved his hand as if there were other scenarios.

"That's sweet."

He flashed her a grin before pulling into the driveway of the house. Before he darted out of his door she grabbed his hand. "I can get my door this time so you don't have to get drenched again."

He nodded as they both exited the vehicle and sprinted towards the front porch. When Kat reached the top step, she turned to see what was taking Ian so long.

She gasped as she watched him flip a hooded figure over his back into the damp grass of the front lawn. The figure kicked out and nailed Ian in the stomach, causing him to take a few steps back. Both men dove at one another and fell to the ground rolling in the mud and slinging punches. Kat opened the front door and yelled for Travis as she took off running towards the fight.

Ian pushed the man off of him but still found himself pinned to the ground. A punch landed in the side of his temple and his vision blurred. He watched as thin, muscular arms wrapped around the man's neck and legs surrounded his middle as Kat leapt onto the man's back to pull him off of Ian.

She gripped her wrist and tightened her chokehold, the man grappling at her arms as he began to choke. He reached over his shoulder and attempted to pull her hair, but he only found air as she ducked out of the way without releasing her grip. Slowly, the man's energy began to wane as he finally collapsed into a heap in the grass. Kat relinquished her hold and scrambled away from him as Ian reached for her and pulled her to him. She crawled towards him as he eased to his knees and she swiped his wet hair out of his face. "Are you okay?" she called over the pounding rain and thunder. Her fingers lightly traced his split lip. He cupped her face and pulled her forehead to his as he took a moment to catch his breath.

Travis sprinted out of the house and slid to his knees beside the hooded man and flipped him on his back and cuffed his wrists before he came to. "What happened?"

Ian shook his head as he stood and pulled Kat to her feet. Travis pulled the man to the porch and called the incident in. Kat walked over and flipped the hood off the man's face.

"Do you know him, Kat?" Travis asked.

She shook her head. "No." She watched as he stirred and he blinked open his eyes, fear flashing before defiance set in and he glared at Kat. Ian took a step towards him and Travis held up his hand. "I've got this, O'Dell. You take Kat inside." Travis held his hand firmly against Ian's chest until Ian finally backed down and reached for Kat's hand as he lead her through the door. When they stepped inside, Ian grabbed her shoulders and looked down. "You will never do that again, Kat, do you hear me?" His eyes flared and her back stiffened.

"If I hadn't, you would still be fighting or worse. Was I just supposed to stand there and let him kill you?"

"He wasn't going to kill me."

"You don't know that. And I will not apologize for helping. I wasn't going to stand there and watch him beat you." Her voice began to rise as her hands began to shake. It was then Ian realized how shaken up she really was. He sighed heavily as he pulled her into his arms and her head rested against his chest, the mud in her hair and along her skin evidence of the struggle she endured on behalf of him. He kissed her wet hair. "I'm sorry, Kat. Thank you, for what you did. But please, don't scare me like that again."

She pulled her face away from his chest and looked up at him, her eyes softening. "I'll try not to. As long as you don't go picking fights." Her lips twitched as he chuckled and pulled her in another tight hug before releasing her.

«CHAPTER SEVEN»

KAT TOOK A TENTATIVE bite of her lasagna as she watched Ian and Travis say the last of their goodbyes to their fellow officers and the chief. Sara nudged her in the shoulder as they sat side by side at the kitchen bar. "You okay?"

Kat nodded as she set her fork down. The task of making dinner had given her time to think as she watched Ian talking in hushed tones with Travis.

"You're awfully quiet." Sara replied, watching Kat closely.

"Just thinking."

"About what?" Sara continued.

Kat turned towards Sara in exasperation. "Plenty. Too many things at once."

"Were you hurt? How's your shoulder?"

"I'm fine. Sore, but fine." Her words finished in a hushed whisper as Ian and Travis walked towards them. Ian's sharp green gaze bore into her and she nudged her plate away for fear of being clumsy.

"We need to talk." His voice was direct, his gaze hard, and his shoulders tense.

"Okay." Kat slid from the bar stool and walked towards the living room area and sat on the couch as Ian sat across from her on the coffee table. He leaned forward and braced his elbows on his knees as he spoke. "You were stupid this evening, Kat. I don't think I have to tell you that, but I need to."

"Stupid?!" Her voice rose and he tampered it down by gently clasping her hand in his.

"I'm not meaning to insult you, okay? Just listen to me." He felt her give into his request by her acquiescence of allowing him to hold her hand. "I had the man under control." He held up a hand to ward off her interruption. She snapped her lips shut again and waited. "You should not have run out there and attacked the guy. For one, you are not an armed, nor trained, officer of the law and shouldn't be doing anything remotely close to that, and second, there could have been another man lingering behind waiting to snatch or harm you. While I was distracted, you were easy pickings, and running head on into a situation is not safe."

"I knew what I was doing," she countered. "And you did not have it under control. I saw him land a blow to your temple."

His eyes narrowed recalling the moment and he noted the worry in her eyes.

"You can say what you want, but you did not recover from that hit as fast as you think. He would have had you pummeled and unconscious if he landed another one to your head like that. I was merely a distraction. Besides, I took self-defense classes for a purpose. I am not going to let some stupid thug threaten my friends or me. I would have been a coward to just stand by and watch you be beaten."

He smirked at the fire in her spirit and the intensity in which she spoke. "I appreciate you coming to help me, but it cannot happen again. Again, Starr and I were not as diligent as we should have been. The chief has assigned two officers to patrol around the house throughout the night. Tomorrow we will be meeting to figure out the next steps. Clearly, having you here with us means nothing to these guys."

"Do we know who the guy is yet? Is he one of Biggs' men? Or Marshall's?" she asked.

"Not sure yet. The guy clammed up once he came to. We will be interviewing him tomorrow though."

Kat reached out and lightly brushed her fingers over his forehead and settled her hand on his cheek. Ian froze as he waited for whatever she planned next, surprised at her tender touch. "You should get some rest, Ian. You look terrible."

His chest rumbled as a soft laugh escaped his lips, then he leaned back and let her hand fall to her side. "Thanks for being so honest, Kat."

She shrugged. "It's what I do."

They both stood and made their way back to the kitchen as Travis and Sara continued eating their dinner. Kat handed Ian a full plate of lasagna before reaching for her own. "Now that we've gotten all of the excitement out of the way," she began, "tell me what you found out about the necklace."

∞

Kat sat silently, her eyes wide as she listened to Travis. "Two hundred and fifty thousand dollars?!" exclaimed Sara. "Why on Earth would Marshall give such an expensive piece of jewelry to Kat?"

"That is what we are trying to figure out," Ian stated, noting the pale tone to Kat's skin as she took a deep breath.

"I had no idea." Her voice was barely above a whisper.

"Don't worry, Kat. We know you didn't know." Travis continued. "We are just trying to figure out where Marshall received such a large amount of money and why he was trying to hide it with you. Any ideas? Think back to when he gave it to you. Did he seem nervous? Was he forceful?"

She shook her head. "No. He gave that to me when things were actually going well. I would say about six months into the relationship or so."

"How long did you two date?" Ian asked.

"Only about a year. A little less."

"So, six months into the relationship he gives you a diamond necklace, and you do not think that is odd?" Ian's tone was edged with suspicion.

"Not really," Kat replied honestly. "Marshall was always a bit over the top with his gifts. He sent me flowers at least once a week. He bought me earrings. Tickets to the theatre. You name it, he gifted it."

"But a diamond necklace?" Ian reiterated.

"Yes," Kat straightened her shoulders and sighed. "Look, I am not the type of woman that is normally doted on. It was nice, at the beginning. After about a few months, I grew tired of all the attention and asked him to stop. He didn't. That's when things grew weird, and I began to really look into why he might be buying me gifts."

"And when did he give you the necklace?"

"My first night of Chicago's Best."

"What is that?" Ian asked.

"The Chicago's Best Awards are a city-wide award ceremony where businesses are given awards voted on by the residents of Chicago," Sara explained. "Kat was nominated that year, well every year since she opened, but that was her first year."

"So he gave you the necklace to wear to the event?" Ian continued.

"No, actually, he gave it to me and specifically asked me not to wear it there. Which I thought was odd at the time, but just wrote it off as one of his weird requests. But now that I think about it, I wonder why?"

Ian and Travis exchanged a look. "Who all goes to this event?" Ian asked.

"It's sort of a who's who among the city of Chicago," Sara explained. "Everyone is there."

"As in city officials?"

"Yes. Business owners, the mayor, the ADA, the police chief... you name it, they are there." Sara waved her hand as if the list continued.

"Then Marshall did not want other high officials seeing you in the necklace," Ian pointed out.

"I guess." Kat shrugged. "Could be he just didn't want me to wear it."

"I doubt it," Travis said. "Men like Marshall like to show off their treasures. Something like a diamond necklace he would want to show off, unless he couldn't."

Ian rubbed a hand over the back of his neck. "When is the next award ceremony?"

"A couple of weeks."

Ian flashed a surprised stare at her. "A couple of weeks?"

She nodded.

He smiled and looked to Travis. "This is perfect. Are you attending?"

"Of course I am. I'm up for Business of the Year again. Though I don't like to brag." She blew on her knuckles and rubbed them on her shoulder in jest.

"Are you thinking what I think you are thinking, O'Dell?" Travis asked with a scowl.

"Yep. Kat needs to wear that necklace." Ian nodded towards Kat and frowned as she shook her head.

"No way. It's ugly."

Sara gasped. "Kat, it is beautiful."

"No, it isn't. It's gaudy and completely not my style. I only kept it because it was made of diamonds. Let Sara wear it."

"Sara is not the target," Ian pointed out. "You are. Imagine Marshall's panic when he sees you walk in with it on."

"I'm to be bait?" Kat asked, crossing her arms in displeasure.

"No, the necklace is," Ian corrected. "Thompson catches one glimpse of that necklace and he will be sweating bullets all night. Something tells me all we would need to do is follow him around and he will lead us straight to Biggs."

"You have high hopes," Travis muttered, not liking the idea of Kat wearing the necklace.

"It's the only way. You know Biggs will have men at this banquet. They spot the necklace. They corner Thompson. Bam. We're there to intercept." Ian clapped his hands and stood, taking his empty plate back to the kitchen. "It's a good plan. I'll tell the chief."

"Whoa, wait a minute." Travis held up his hand. "I don't want to put Kat in that kind of danger."

"She wouldn't be in danger, Starr." Ian blew a frustrated sigh as he placed his hands on his hips. "We'll provide protective detail to her all night."

"And how do you propose we do that?" Travis asked.

"One of us is to be her date." He grinned and nodded towards Kat. She dropped her forehead into her hand and groaned. Ian's smile faded. "What? You don't want Starr or me as your date?"

"Travis is Sara's date, because she is up for Business of the Year as well," Kat explained.

"Okay," Ian shrugged his shoulders. "I don't see the problem."

"That means you will have to be my date, and I always take Jeremiah. He's a staple of the café. People love him and they know him. It would be wrong of me not to take him."

"I'm sure he would understand, Kat. Besides, he can still come. I'm sure I can talk to the people in charge and explain what is going on-"

"What? No." Travis held up a hand. "No one can know. You know how many people Thompson is friends with? Look, O'Dell, I know you are new around here, so let me be the one to take lead on this. I will talk to the chief and see what he says. Until then, Kat, just continue planning as if Jeremiah were your date."

Ian frowned, his disappointment evident as he turned to walk back into the kitchen to rinse his plate.

"It could work," Kat mumbled, looking at Travis. "No matter how much we do not like the idea, it sounds like our best plan."

Travis reached across the table and squeezed her hand. "We'll think of something else, Kat. I'm not going to put you in harm's way."

She smiled and squeezed his hand in return. "You're sweet, Trav, but I'm okay with this plan. I know it can work. Talk to the chief; tell him I am agreeing to the plan. See what he says."

"I don't like it." Travis sighed as he nodded that he would follow her wishes. "But I'll talk to O'Dell and the chief. How do you think Jeremiah will take it?"

"Not sure. He does enjoy going. Maybe I can somehow swing an invitation for him as well."

"I'll see what I can do. Surely the chief will have a way. How do you feel about O'Dell being your date?" Travis winked and accepted the punch to his arm that Sara gave him.

Rolling her eyes, Kat stood. "Nothing like a night out on the town with a determined detective and wearing a house around my neck."

∞

Ian stood just inside the kitchen archway listening to Travis and Kat discuss the awards ceremony. Kat seemed disappointingly uninterested in attending as his date. *For the best*, he thought. His job would be to protect her, so his notion of anything more would have no place on the big night. She looked up at him as he walked back towards the table. "You win, O'Dell. I'll let you date me."

His lips twitched before he allowed the smile to shine through. "I'm so relieved."

"Only for one night though," Kat clarified. "I've got a reputation to uphold."

"And what reputation is that?" Sara asked on a laugh.

"A woman about town, Sara, duh."

Travis and Sara burst into laughter, Kat waving away their disbelief.

"Yeah, right." Travis said. "If anything, your reputation is that you do not have time for romance."

Kat shrugged. "That might be true." She flashed a quick grin towards Ian. "But I like to think of myself as a hot commodity."

"Maybe your chocolate chip muffins." Travis winced at the punch he received in his shoulder.

"Keep it up, Starr," Kat teased once more before growing serious. "In all honesty, though, I do have a couple of concerns."

Ian pulled out his chair and sat. "Go ahead. I want to hear them. I do not want you to be nervous about the plan."

"Well for starters, how are we going to make it seem like you are truly my date? I mean, Marshall is going to know something is amiss. I walk in wearing the diamond necklace and a cop as my date? Even I don't think he is that stupid, and trust me, I question his brain capacity all the time."

"We will just have to make our relationship seem genuine," Ian pointed out. "Is it that far-fetched? You're best friends with Travis, a detective, and I am his roommate. Perhaps people will think it just evolved from our friendship." The explanation sounded simple enough when he said it, Kat thought, but deep down she knew Marshall would not buy into their façade unless they were truly convincing.

"You do not look appeased." Ian waited for her to continue, her brow furrowed in concentration.

"I'm not. It's not that easy. Marshall has eyes everywhere. If I were seeing someone, he would know well before the awards ceremony."

Sara snapped her fingers. "The flowers."

"What?" Travis turned to her in question.

"Kat received that bouquet of flowers from a secret admirer. What if we pretended they were from Ian? Then the idea of something evolving does not seem so out of reach. People will just assume."

"Except the real person who sent them," Kat reminded them. "And what if that was Marshall?"

"Then I should send you some. Publicly. Have them delivered to the café during a busy time." Ian grabbed his cell phone out of his pant pocket and entered a reminder. "Several advances like that and people will believe there's more than friendship between us."

Kat leaned back in her chair on a sigh, disappointment washed over her face.

"What other concerns do you have, Kat?" Travis asked.

"None that warrant me voicing them aloud."

"No, we want to hear them," Ian pressed.

Her eyes briefly narrowed in frustration before she continued. "I just don't like lying to everyone. It's frustrating. I pride myself on my character and here I am coming up with a master plan to try and convince, not one person, but an entire city, that I am dating a detective. Just so I can attend the one event I look forward to every year and continue said lie throughout the entire evening. How am I supposed to enjoy myself? How am I supposed to act? It all seems so false, and I don't like feeling that way."

"You're helping catch one of the biggest drug leaders in the country, Kat. I think people will understand," Travis stated.

"No, Travis, I am trying to catch Marshall doing something. This has no connection to Biggs."

"Not true," Ian interrupted. "Thompson is the key in all of this. I know he is. We just have to catch him. The threats on your life stem from your connection to him. And I guarantee you, they are because of that necklace. This event is our best chance to draw Biggs out and his connection to Thompson. If you do not want to do this, you need to tell us now so we can prepare another way. Either way, we have to uncover their connection in order to keep you safe."

"I said I would do it, so I am. I am just putting it on record that I do not like it." She crossed her arms and nervously bit the inside of her lips.

Ian reached over and lightly grabbed one of her hands, causing her arms to uncross and fall to her lap. He threaded his fingers through hers and she could not help the slight jump in her pulse at the contact, another frustrating reaction she wished did not exist. "I will not let anything happen to you, Kat. Your safety is our first priority. If at any point I feel your safety has been compromised, we will leave. Understand?"

She nodded.

"Good." He flashed his killer smile as he leaned back in his chair and gave her hand one last squeeze before he turned his attention back to Travis.

"Well O'Dell, I guess tomorrow you will start courting Kat." He chuckled at the look of dismay on his friend's face. "And perhaps in a couple of weeks you two will have the entire city eating out of the palm of your hands."

Kat raised her hand slightly. "One more thing."

Both men groaned and she flashed a wicked smile towards Sara.

"What is it, Kat?"

"Well, since I am participating in this plot strictly for the benefit of the police department, does this mean my dress is at the cost of said police department?"

Sara grinned and turned to hear Travis' response.

He shook his head as he laughed. "Sure. Whatever dress you want, it's on us."

"Done." She clapped her hands and hopped to her feet. "I think this will be fun. Oh, and Ian, you will need to wear a tuxedo. Not a suit. And it has to be black." She lightly tapped him on the shoulder as she passed to walk towards the kitchen.

"We've been fake dating for two seconds and she's already trying to change my wardrobe," Ian mumbled, making them all laugh.

"I heard that, O'Dell," Kat called from the kitchen, a smile in her tone.

∞

Jeremiah barged into the kitchen with a frown on his face as he rested his palms on Kat's worktable.

"What is the matter, Jer?" Kat asked, looking up from her work of kneading bread dough.

"Your fr- boyfriend," he corrected. "He has been coming in here every couple of hours and he lingers right next to the counter. His badge fully visible. It's making the customers nervous."

"Why would it make them nervous?"

"I don't know. Probably because there have been several incidents that have taken place here. Scares them into thinking perhaps they should rethink coming here."

"Don't be dramatic." Kat wiped her hands on a towel and then moved the dough pans towards the opposite counter.

"I'm not, Kat. We've had over ten customers turn and leave without even considering placing an order. You have Ian near the counter. Smithens at the North entrance. Two officers out front. Can you blame them?"

"We've had customers leave?" Concern laced her voice as she looked up and finally gave him her full attention.

"Yes." He relaxed now that she seemed to take his words seriously.

She tossed the towel over her shoulder. "I'll handle it."

She walked out of the kitchen, Jeremiah hot on her heels as she directed her steps towards Ian, fire in her eyes. Ian looked up and his smile wavered as he noted the quiet anger seeping from her aura. Thinking fast, when she reached him, he lightly grabbed her chin and quickly placed his lips over hers. The kiss was quick and light and over way too soon in his book, and it did exactly what he had hoped: distracted Kat enough to tamper down some of her temper. "W-what was that?" Her voice was a whisper as she nervously looked around and caught several customers smirking in her direction.

"Sorry, I just wanted to capture some of that fire for myself." He winked and she lightly shoved his shoulder.

"Stop being cute," she ordered, wagging her finger in his face.

"I'll try." He gently grabbed her hand and she yanked it free. "Stop it, O'Dell, I'm trying to scold you."

He could see her resolve slipping as he held up his hands in innocence. "Very well. Scold away."

She placed her hands on her narrow hips. "Jeremiah said that customers have been leaving due to the police presence lurking about. You're intimidating my customers. Can we please get rid of some of the officers?"

"No."

His answer was short and left no room for argument.

"Well, then could they please wear regular clothes so they blend in better?" Kat asked.

He tilted his head.

She gently grabbed his hand this time. "Please, Ian. I do not want my business to suffer anymore than it already has."

Looking into her eyes, Ian found himself nodding. "Fine. I'll have them rotate patrols and change into civilian clothes."

Smiling, Kat clapped her hands and then threw her arms around his neck and kissed his cheek. "Thank you."

He slipped his arms around her waist, and she nervously hopped out of his arms. "I should get back to work." She darted back towards the kitchen leaving him disappointed.

Jeremiah slid him a cup of coffee. "You're acting skills are pretty on point. Or are you really even acting?" He teased, as he wiped down the counter with a damp towel.

Ian grunted as he took a sip of his coffee.

"Look, man, I get it. You're trying to make it seem like you're doing your job for this whole Thompson shake down. But let's be honest, we all see how you look at her."

"What?" Ian asked.

"It's obvious you are genuinely interested in Kat."

"Is that so?"

Jeremiah rolled his eyes. "Yes. Now do you want my help or not?"

Ian waited a minute and noted Jeremiah's pointed gaze. "Fine."

A wide smile spread over Jeremiah's face. "Ha. I knew it." He held up his hands at Ian's frustrated groan. "Okay, okay, I won't rub it in." Laughing, he nudged a sheet of paper towards Ian. "A list of restaurants Kat loves and some of her favorite things."

Ian perused the list. "Do you know her favorite flower?"

"No. All I know is it is *not* carnations. But Sara would probably know better than I would. Also, if you're going to send her flowers, don't do a big overly gaudy arrangement. Kat's not really into big and gaudy."

"I got that impression." Ian mumbled.

"And you might want to hold off on the kissing."

Ian flushed and Jeremiah laughed. "I mean it was fun to see Kat completely surprised and knocked off her feet, but she's also not one for public displays of affection."

"Got it."

The kitchen door opened and Kat walked out, both men straightening and avoiding one another as if they had not been talking. She walked towards Ian and nudged a bright green box towards him. "For you to take to the station."

"Thanks. How did you know I was about to leave?"

"You always leave around this time."

"I didn't think you noticed."

"I may be in the back most of the time, but I keep tabs on my place enough to know when my regulars leave."

"I'm a regular now?" He asked with a grin.

She leaned over the counter and folded down his disheveled shirt collar, her fingers lightly brushing his neck. When she retreated, she smiled.

"Thanks."

"Don't mention it. Gotta make sure my man looks good." She winked as a relieved laugh escaped his lips.

"Right. Well, I guess I will be on my way. I'll be back at-"

"Six. I know, remember?" She tapped her temple and he smiled.

"Of course. Have a good day, Kat."

"You too, sugar muffin." He paused and turned back around. "You're right... I need to work on that one. Just testing it out."

Laughing, he shook his head as he turned and left.

"Sugar muffin?" Jeremiah asked in disgust.

"I thought it would be funny." Kat laughed as Jeremiah just continued shaking his head and face palmed her to nudge her back towards the kitchen. Playfully, she swatted at his hand as she retreated back into her domain.

«CHAPTER EIGHT»

A WEEK OF DEAD LEADS passed, and Ian found himself standing on a pedestal surrounded by mirrors. He pulled at the cuff on his jacket.

"Looking sharp," Travis whistled, as he exited a fitting room and waited while the tailor made marks on Ian's back.

"It's been awhile since I've worn a tuxedo." Ian pulled at the collar of his shirt and the tailor swatted his hand away to insert a pin.

"Kat will appreciate the extra effort." Travis eyed the shoes Ian had picked out and slipped his own foot in one to test them out. Disliking the fit, he nudged it off and continued walking around in his socks. "So how has the fauxmance gone?"

Ian's brow rose in his reflection as he looked up at Travis. "Fauxmance?"

"Yeah, you and Kat. Have you romanced her the last week?"

"Shouldn't you be asking her that?"

"Why would I ask Kat?"

"Because she is on the receiving end of all my efforts." The tailor slid the jacket off of Ian's shoulders and set it aside.

Travis crossed his arms. "You mean she hasn't done anything for you?"

Ian shrugged. "Did we expect her to? The whole plan was for people to think I was her boyfriend, for people to see me doting upon her."

"Yeah, but she had to have reciprocated at some point." At Ian's blank stare, Travis' mouth dropped open. "She hasn't done anything?"

"We are able to maintain appearances when she comes out of the kitchen to the front counter and I'm there."

"That's it?"

"Should there be more?" Ian looked confused.

"Well, yeah. I thought you two would put forth more effort."

"I've put forth effort," Ian defended, turning around and facing Travis. "I've made sure to maintain a respectable, professional distance while appearing to be the adoring boyfriend."

"Right. I'll ask some of the regulars and see what they think."

"What? How are you going to do that without it seeming suspicious?"

"Trust me, I won't even have to ask some of them. They will ask me about you. Kat has loyal customers. Some of her oldest customers have been after her to commit to someone for years now. If she has a new man in her life, they would know."

Ian turned back around as the tailor offered up several choices and styles of ties. "No bow tie." Ian waved away several of the choices and the tailor silently slinked away to retrieve more options. "Just be subtle," Ian warned Travis.

"I always am." He grinned as Ian's disbelief showed in his hard stare.

Ian's cell phone rang and he slid it out of his pocket and held the screen up in the mirror so

Travis could see the caller. He then answered it. "Hey, Kat."

∞

Kat sat on a stool at the main counter and watched as Jeremiah added whipped cream to a Frappuccino as she waited for Ian to answer his phone. She twirled the long stems of the three tulips in her fingers, the pale yellow ribbon tied in a loose bow. The three bold, orange flowers a sweet gesture. She knew it was for their act, but part of her enjoyed the sweetness. She much preferred the simplicity of a small cluster of blooms over a giant bouquet. His voice came through the line.

"Hey," she greeted. "What are you doing?"

"I'm currently being poked and prodded. I'm getting my suit ordered."

"Perfect. I was meaning to remind you to do that." She smiled into the phone as she heard the tailor ask him a question.

"To what do I owe the pleasure of your phone call?" Ian asked.

Kat's smile widened as she looked at the flowers. "I was calling to thank you."

"For what?"

Katharine E. Hamilton

"The flowers." She heard him pause. She had never called to thank him before. For the chocolates he had sent last week, the ice cream cone from her favorite sweet shop, or even her favorite pizza from Tony's down the street. But something about the simple flowers stirred her in a way nothing else had.

"Oh." He was silent. "You're welcome. I hoped I guessed your favorite. Was I close?"

"Nailed it."

"Good." She heard the grin in his voice.

An awkward silence hung over the phone line, as neither of them knew how to follow up their conversation.

Kat cleared her throat. "That's all I wanted. I'll let you get back."

"Kat-" Ian called quickly before she hung up.

"Yes?"

Her eager response had him nervously run a hand through his shaggy hair. *He needed a trim*, he realized, staring into the mirrors.

"Ian?" Her voice rang through the line again and had him shaking his head.

Katharine E. Hamilton

"Sorry." He muttered into the phone as he looked over his shoulder to see where Travis stood. Seeing his friend further inside the shop looking at suit jackets, he turned back to his conversation. "I, um... would you like to do dinner tonight?

Silence on the other end had him fidgeting and kicking himself for even encouraging the idea.

"I would like that."

Wait, his sharp green gaze hit the mirrors, *she said yes.* He smiled. "Great. I will see you at-"

"Six." She confirmed on a grin. "Later, baby cakes." A pause. "Yeah, that one isn't a good one either, is it?"

He chuckled and he heard her giggle before she hung up. He slid his phone back into his pocket and stepped off the platform.

"What did Kat want?" Travis asked.

"To thank me." Ian unbuttoned the crisp white button up shirt and slipped it off and handed it to the expecting hands of the tailor.

"For what?"

"I sent her a few flowers."

"A few flowers? As in a bouquet? Or literally a few flowers?"

"A few."

"And she called to thank you?" Travis asked.

"Yep."

"Wow. I'm impressed. First that you knew she liked the simpler things, and second, that she called to talk to you about it. She's normally awkward with stuff like that. And way to go, having it delivered during the day so people will see it."

Ian tried to stifle down his frustration but his frown only caused Travis to smile even more. "Ah, I see that aggravates you. When exactly did your gifts stop being an act?"

"It doesn't matter."

"Clearly it does."

"I'm done here, Starr. You find your suit?"

"Don't change the subject." Travis badgered, as Ian brushed passed him towards the front entrance.

"Enough, Starr," Ian growled as they both hopped inside his truck. He distracted himself with driving as Travis continued to babble on about Kat and her lack of interest in relationships. The topic annoyed Ian. "I think that is enough of an education, Travis. Thanks."

Travis stopped when he heard the tone of Ian's voice. "Look, man, I'm just trying to help you out. Kat is not good with relationships and that is why she avoids them. I mean, look at Marshall Thompson. Talk about a bad situation there."

"I'm not Marshall Thompson."

"Ah, so you are genuinely interested in her." Travis smirked. "I could tell."

"It doesn't matter. Like you said, she is not looking for a relationship, so what is the point?"

"Not to mention you would be breaking almost every protocol in the book for this case if you pursued her."

"I know."

"Course, once we settle this case the topic of a relationship could come about. If you're still interested in her by then." Travis studied Ian's face from the corner of his eye and noted the harsh lines of disappointment.

"First priority is the case," Ian stated, his tone telling Travis their conversation was over.

"Right." Travis agreed softly so as not to upset his partner further. He waited as Ian found a parking spot along the street near Kat's café and they both made their way towards the door. A line of people curved from inside and down part of the sidewalk, business thriving due to the outdoor movie on the side of the Connelly Building down the street. The once a month tradition, a free event where people could picnic and watch old films outside, always brought a fair share of business to Kat. And by the looks of it, she would not be leaving at her usual six o' clock hour. They slid through the door, shouldering past people until they reached the counter. Jeremiah glanced up with a nod. Travis took a seat on a stool as Ian sidestepped more people and ducked under the counter bar door. "I'm going in back," he told Jeremiah. Jeremiah didn't even look up, just sent a small wave over his shoulder that he had heard him.

When Ian opened the swinging door, voices carried, mainly Kat's as she directed several workers in different tasks. He watched her for a minute as she quickly prepared several dishes and then tweaked the other dishes as well before ringing the bell on the wall for one of the outside waiters to come pick up. She then grabbed two more order slips and quickly began working on more plates. The other two workers, college-aged girls, looked up as he entered. Kat barked an order, and not hearing a response, looked up at the girls. She then turned towards the door to see what had distracted them. She smiled and rolled her eyes before turning back to the girls and clapping her hands. Both girls blushed as they listened to her directions and set about getting back to work. Kat then wiped her hands on a towel and walked over.

She slipped her arms around his waist and hugged him. "A handsome face walks in and we all lose our minds," she teased, as she lightly kissed his cheek. He held her a moment longer, relishing the closeness before he let her slip away.

"I have bad news," she said.

"You're extremely busy and cannot do dinner," he finished. "I sort of figured that out." Though he was disappointed, he acted as if he were completely fine.

"No."

Her response had his gaze looking down into hers. "Oh. I thought since-"

She grinned. "I just may be a few minutes later than six."

A relieved smile washed over his face and she found the sight appealing.

"Take your time. I'll just wait out here." He turned to leave and felt her grasp his hand. He turned around and she leaned up on her tiptoes and graced another kiss along his cheek.

"I might as well rub it in, right?" she asked quietly, nodding over her shoulder to the two wide-eyed college girls. He smirked and tapped her nose with his finger. "Cute, Riesling. Cute." Letting her hand slide from his he exited the kitchen. She stood

Katharine E. Hamilton

there a moment and pondered just removing her apron and leaving right then, but she knew she had to help the girls get somewhat ahead on all the orders before she left them to fend for themselves. Turning back to her work and the curious glances from her staff, she worked quickly so she could leave and enjoy an evening with Ian.

∞

Ian glanced at his watch as the kitchen door opened and Kat stepped out. She hung her apron on the hook by the door. "I'm ready when you are, O'Dell."

Jeremiah looked up as Kat patted him on the back. "Everything should be good to go back there. The girls are caught up."

"I'm sure we can handle it, Kat. Go home." Jeremiah tugged on the edges of her ponytail before turning her shoulders and nudging her Ian's direction.

"I'm not going home," she stated with a smile. "I'm going to dinner with my sexy boyfriend." Her words carried towards Ian and he looked up and smiled as she walked towards him and linked her arm in his. "If you need me, don't call."

Jeremiah shook his head on a chuckle and turned back to his customers. Kat looked up at Ian as they walked towards the door. "Where were you thinking for dinner?"

"That is up to you. I had thought about Giliano's."

Her face lit up. "That does sound delicious." She looked down at her wardrobe. "Though sadly I'm not really dressed nicely."

"I was thinking along the lines of take out," Ian admitted. Again, her face spread into an easy smile. "Dinner and a movie at your place?"

Surprised, she looked up at him. "My place? You mean I can stay there again?"

He shook his head. "No. But I figured you might like to enjoy it a bit and have a quiet evening there."

"I would. You're getting good at this whole boyfriend sweetness." Kat laughed as he opened her door and she slid into his truck. He slid behind the wheel and began navigating the city streets towards the restaurant. "So how was your day of tuxedo fitting and crime fighting?" Kat asked.

"I felt rather 007 actually." He liked the small snort and giggle he received as her response.

"Nice one, James Bond. Any leads on Marshall?"

He shook his head, his smile fading into a firm line. "I am trying to connect a few dots, but it really does boil down to the awards ceremony."

"Unless something turns up before then," she added.

"There is that, but we have to hope there will be no other incidents involving you."

"It's been rather quiet on that front, so that's a good sign. I've been well protected. I have you guys to thank for that."

"We do our best." He offered an encouraging smile.

"I had one of my oldest customers ask me about you today."

"Is that so?" His brow lifted as he flicked his turn signal to head down a small side street.

"Yes. She is about seventy years old, teaches yoga to senior adults, and stops by every single morning on her way to the studio. Oh, and she has blue hair," Kat explained.

Ian chuckled at her description. "And what did Ms. Blue Hair have to say?"

"She asked about the, and I quote, 'tall glass of sugar and sexy' that had been 'lurking around my apron strings.'"

Bursting into laughter, Ian noted the small blush to Kat's cheeks.

"And what did you say?"

"At first I tried to blow it off with a 'Oh you know, they just flock to me like flies,'" she said as she waved her hand nonchalantly. "But then Jeremiah cast me a hard glare and I realized these were the types of opportunities we needed in order for our relationship to seem more viable, so I told her you were my new boyfriend. She was rather excited. In fact, I'm pretty sure she has our entire wedding planned. And probably the name of our firstborn picked out. Just so you know."

Ian continued to laugh and braced himself for the small punch Kat landed in his arm. "Seriously, Ian, this is getting hard. What's going to happen when things return back to normal? I'm going to have to spend time answering even more questions about you. Why did it not work out? What did I do to run off such a guy? Why did I not try harder? So many questions."

"It will be alright, Kat, trust me." He lightly squeezed her hand and did not let go as he turned onto the street leading to the restaurant. She allowed the small luxury of having his warm fingers lace through hers. She allowed the small moment of pleasure even though she knew it was not genuine. He squeezed it one last time before pulling into a parking spot and parking the truck.

Katharine E. Hamilton

He then stepped out and walked around to her side to open the door. A small gesture that also pleased her. *Pretty much everything about Ian pleased her*, she realized. He opened the door to Giliano's, the aroma of Italian spices and fresh bread arousing her hungry stomach. "I think I instantly became hungrier," Kat admitted, as they waited in line to order.

"Smells incredible, I will admit." Ian lightly guided her forward with his hand at the base of her back and let it rest there as he reached for a menu. He opened it for both of them as they stood waiting their turn. She sidled up next to him to view it better and the faint scent of her perfume wafted up to him.

"Kat?"

The voice Kat longed to forget had her stepping closer to Ian before they both looked up to find Marshall Thompson standing before them. He forced a smile at them and Kat looked up to Ian for guidance. Ian smiled politely and extended his hand. "Mr. Thompson, I don't believe we've met. I'm Ian O'Dell."

Marshall returned the handshake in kind, but his gaze remained on Kat. "You're right. I don't believe we have. You're the new detective?"

"I am."

Katharine E. Hamilton

"I remember you from the café a few weeks back and I've heard of your work. Impressive." Thompson continued, his gaze sizing up Ian. "And it's nice to see someone is looking out for Kat."

Ian slid his arm around Kat's waist and pulled her tighter. "I would say it's a bit more than looking out for her." He looked down at her and winked, a small pink blush rose in her cheeks as he lightly kissed her forehead. She placed a hand on his chest and nudged him back as if embarrassed, though she playfully squeezed his side.

Marshall eyed them closely before continuing. "I'm not sure if Travis told you, Kat, but I came by a few weeks ago."

"He mentioned it, but I didn't know what he was talking about so I didn't think much of it. Did you find what you were looking for?" She looked down at the menu briefly as if their conversation was not important, but she felt her hands begin to shake. Ian folded the menu and then pulled her arms around his waist and hugged her close, her hands buried in his jacket as if he planned to hide her jitters.

"No. I'm afraid not," Marshall continued, growing more agitated by the moment.

"Sorry to hear that, and sorry I couldn't help you out." She nodded towards the counter. "Looks like it's our turn. Good night, Marshall." She walked forward with Ian and they ordered two entrees to go. Ian kept a close watch on Marshall out of the corner of his eye until the man walked away in a huff. When Thompson rounded the corner to head back towards his table, Kat relaxed. "Thanks. He makes me nervous," she whispered.

"You did fine." He lightly rubbed her shoulder. "We'll grab our food and keep acting as if his presence doesn't bother us. Then we will take it to your house and continue our evening as planned."

"Do we need to call Travis and tell him?"

"I will send him a text, but there's really nothing we can do at this point. I think he was just looking for a reaction out of you. You didn't give him one."

"Are you sure?" She looked up at him, her brown eyes full of concern. He lightly placed his thumb on her chin and held it in his hand. "You did good, Kat. I only saw your nerves because I was looking for them. He did not notice." She continued to stare into his eyes and he felt himself drawing closer to her. His hand tilted her chin a little higher and his gaze darted to her lips. As he began to close the gap, a bell rang and their order number was called. He dropped his hand and reached forward, grabbing the white bag off the counter. He then grabbed Kat's hand and pulled her outside, inwardly chastising himself for almost letting his affections slip past the professional boundary line he had drawn.

∞

When he pulled into the driveway in front of Travis' house, the silence in the truck carried over to his exiting the vehicle and opening Kat's door. "I guess we are eating here?" she asked, the slight disappointment in her voice shaking him from his brood.

"No. I just wanted to park my truck over here for the night. We can walk over to your place."

Her spirits lightened as she walked to her mailbox and retrieved her mail on their way. He watched her routine of unlocking the door, disarming the alarm, and setting her keys in a small bowl by the front door as they entered. She slipped out of her shoes as well, and he watched as she walked their bag of food to the coffee table. "Want to eat in the living room?" she asked, turning to see him standing near the door. "You okay?" She tilted her head as she studied him, her brow wrinkled.

"Fine. I'm fine," he mumbled as he stepped forward. "This is fine." He waved his hand towards the food.

She watched him as he sat on the edge of the couch and waited for her. "You can relax, you know," she quipped. "I'm not going to bite."

He looked at her confused.

"You look like you're about to bolt out the door at any moment." Kat chuckled as she continued into the kitchen and came back carrying a bottle of red wine and two wide-rimmed glasses.

"I am fine," Ian said again.

"Right, I got that." Kat poured him a glass and handed it to him. "Fine this, fine that, everything is fine, fine, fine." She clinked her glass to his in a toast and sat beside him. She unpacked their boxes of food and handed him his. The small living room was comfortable, the smells of the rich Italian pastas mixed with candles of a lavender and vanilla scent, a scent Ian had come to associate with Kat. The bold colors of the furniture and throw blankets fit her personality as well. The bright blues, yellows, and greens added a sense of informality to the space. The new, mint wall paint a contrast yet fitting color to match. *She had made a home here,* he realized. *A comfortable one.* And he hoped he could help keep it safe. His eyes carried over to the new sliding glass door in the kitchen and his thoughts wandered back to the night she took a cinderblock to the shoulder. "Please stop worrying." Her voice broke his line of thought as he noticed her watching him. "I'm sorry, Kat, I just can't help but think about that door shattering and you being hurt again."

"The odds of someone attacking the same way twice are slim."

"True," he agreed. "But we still need to be vigilant." He rose to his feet, walked towards the door, and pulled the curtains to block the view. He walked back to his place on the couch and sat to eat.

"Feel better?" she asked with a small smile.

"Not really." His response was firm as he forked a mouthful of fettuccini.

Kat lowered her box of food and crossed her arms. "Okay, O'Dell, this is not going to be how we spend our evening. If you're going to act like a detective, then we should just go back to Travis' and let him hover as well. This dinner was supposed to be an escape, was it not?"

He set his food aside as well and looked up. "I apologize, Kat. You're exactly right." He retrieved his badge from his pant pocket and walked it over to the fireplace mantle and left it. He then walked back to his seat. "Detective O'Dell officially benched for the night."

"Good." She grinned as she picked her food back up.

"You still have those carnations? They're looking pretty sad with no one here to water them." Ian pointed towards the mantle once more and Kat shook her head.

"I forgot about those. Remind me to toss them before we leave so they do not begin to mold and smell."

"I think I can do that." He twirled his fork in the cream-laden pasta.

"Now tell me about yourself," Kat said.

"What would you like to know?"

She shrugged. "I don't know. Something personal. As of right now I don't really know much about you other than what you do for a living. Where are you originally from?"

"Born and raised in Indiana."

"Indiana?" she asked in surprise.

"Yep."

"What made you move here?"

"Just navigated my way from one precinct to another until I found one that fit well. I like Chicago, and would like to make a career here."

"Do your parents still live in Indiana?" Kat asked.

"No. They now live in Chicago as well."

"Really?" Her brows lifted. "What do they do for a living?"

"My father is a professor at the University of Chicago and my mother stays at home. She's an avid knitter and teaches classes at several different craft shops throughout the city."

"Cute," Kat said. "I do not know how to knit, that is for sure. Sara tends to be the craftier of the two of us."

"And what of your family? Where does *the* Kat Riesling stem from?" He smirked as her smile softened and her eyes melted into soft pools of warm chocolate.

"My parents live in Tennessee."

"Is that where you are from?"

She shook her head. "No, I was born here in Chicago. My dad is a retired police chief and my mom is a retired teacher."

"Police chief?" Ian asked, his tone surprised.

Kat laughed. "Yes, which may explain why Travis rats me out to the current one all the time. Chief Winters is close to my dad."

"I imagine so." Ian took a sip of his wine. "So how do you feel about law enforcement since you were raised around it?"

"What do you mean?"

He flushed a bit around the collar and she found the sight endearing. *He was asking how she felt about him*, she realized. "I like it," she answered. "It's dangerous, sure, but I like the integrity that comes with it. My dad lived and breathed his work, but he was also great at separating his work from home. He was quite disappointed when I decided not to go into law enforcement. However, he was extremely pleased when Travis and I became such good friends. Makes him think I'm being looked after."

"Do they visit you often?"

"Not as often as any of us would like."

"Have you told them what is going on?"

"I didn't have to. I'm friends with Travis, remember? He can't keep a secret to save his life."

"And your father didn't come up here the instant he found out you were in danger?"

"I talked him down. I bragged about the skills of this new detective I know, and how amazing he is at protecting me. He seemed convinced I was in good hands." She winked.

"Wow, yeah that detective guy sure sounds awesome."

She playfully shoved his shoulder but smiled. "He is, once you get to know him."

Ian's face sobered and he turned to find her closer than he realized. She took a sip of her wine. "Tell me something else about you, Detective O'Dell."

"Why don't you ask me what you would like to know? It is hard to think of something interesting on the spot."

"Fair enough." Kat crossed her legs under her and faced him, her knee lightly brushing against his thigh as she forked another mouthful of her pasta. "What's your favorite color?"

"Seriously?" He laughed. "That's the best you can come up with?"

"Hey, you put me on the spot, what was I supposed to do?"

He lightly tickled her knee and she fidgeted.

"It's green," he answered. "And what is your favorite color, Riesling? By the looks of it you dabble with pretty much every shade in the spectrum." He motioned to her living room.

"Green as well. Though blue is a close second. All shades. Except neon. I'm not a fan of neon colors."

He tried to wipe the smile off of his face and then shook his head. "Why don't you tell me why you opened the café?"

Beaming, Kat set her food aside and clapped her hands. "Now we're talking. That's a great question, O'Dell. Good job."

He pretended to bow as she topped off her glass. She gestured toward his and he nodded and watched as she poured the deep red liquid.

"When I was a little girl, my grandmother owned a small diner here in Chicago. My dad would drop me off there during the summers and I would help her out. Mostly cleaning in those days because I was too small to contribute much else. But I remember everything about the place. The smells, the colors, the people... it was amazing. I just remember thinking to myself that one day I would do the same thing. I wanted to bring joy to people. Food has an amazing way of bringing people together. Actually, I have learned that coffee has an even bigger impact, but food as well. I love interacting with the city in such an intimate way. I provide a step in someone's morning routine. I like having that role, that chance to impact their day somehow."

He listened and watched as her eyes glassed over as she spoke, her mind picturing each customer that ventured through her café. Jeremiah. Her kitchen. He saw the spark in her eyes when she continued sharing story after story about individual customers, her employees, and of course, her cats. Her enthusiasm and joy were contagious, and they radiated off of her in the glow of her face. Before he could think twice, he silenced her words with his lips on hers. She froze, and he pulled away just slightly so as to gauge her reaction. When she did not say anything, he closed the gap once more. He felt her relax as he gently cupped her face in his hand and glided his lips over hers. She placed a hand on his chest and gently nudged him back, his hold on her lips breaking, and his hand touching air before he dropped it to his side.

"Kat, I-"

Before he could apologize, a piercing sound buzzed through the air and the lamp next to Kat shattered. He quickly grabbed her by the shoulders and dove towards her, knocking her off of the couch and onto the floor as a spray of bullets burst through the front window and erupted through the room. Ian reached for his phone out of his pocket and pressed it to his ear barking orders to whoever graced the other line. Kat closed her eyes and held firmly to Ian's shirt as he hunkered over her, glass, food, and furniture stuffing flying through the air as bullets slammed into her belongings.

The air grew quiet. Then the subtle sounds of sirens on the horizon emerged. Kat shifted.

"Stay down, Kat. We are not moving until my guys come through that door."

She gripped the front of his shirt and he looked down at her. He smoothed the hair out of her eyes and gently brushed his knuckles over her cheek. "Are you hurt?"

"No." Her voice was barely a whisper and her eyes were wide.

He tucked her hair behind her ear. "Good. Just hang in there, all right? Back up is almost here."

She closed her eyes and he saw a silent tear drip from the corner of her eye. He brushed it away with his thumb, but Kat did not respond. She patiently waited until the door slamming open broke the silence and chaos ruled her house.

«CHAPTER NINE»

SARA HANDED KAT A glass of water, the quiet of Travis' house settling her somewhat rattled nerves as she escaped the madness of her home and the event that had just taken place.

"You sure you are doing okay?" Sara asked.

Kat nodded. "I'm fine. Thanks for this." Kat took a long sip of the water and let the cold liquid soothe her parched throat. "Any word from the guys?"

"Not yet. Travis stuck his head in here a few minutes ago to tell me the chief was on his way to speak to you."

"Oh joy," Kat mumbled looking down at her hands wrapped around the cool glass.

"Travis didn't seem too happy about you guys even being at the house. Last I saw him he was yelling at Ian," Sara reported.

"It wasn't his fault. It could have happened here just as much as it could have there."

"True, but Travis still isn't happy."

"I'm sure Ian is beating himself up over it enough. He doesn't need Travis beating him too," Kat warned.

Sara studied her a moment. "You really like him, don't you?"

Kat looked into Sara's understanding gaze and nodded. "Yeah, I do. He's a great guy, Sara. And he truly cares about whether or not I'm safe. In fact, before the crazy shooting fiasco, I was having an amazing time with him. We were laughing, getting to know one another... he kissed me."

"He kissed you?!" Sara asked with wide eyes and a sly grin. "My, my, my, Kat, do tell."

Kat playfully shoved her. "It was nice. I could tell it took him by surprise too, but overall it was a happy surprise. And then bullets started coming through the windows."

"Oh Kat, I'm so sorry." Sara patted her thigh. "I'm sure it was special to him, though, and that as soon as he wraps up everything over there he will want to pick up where you guys left off."

"I'm not sure it's a good idea if we did."

"Why not?" Sara looked up as Kat stood and began to pace.

"Because we got distracted. We should have kept our guard up. We should have known something like this would happen. Ian even warned me and I convinced him we would be fine. So stupid." She shook her head in disgust as the front door swung open and Travis, Ian, and Chief Winters entered. Ian met her gaze, but no hint of his feelings showed and Kat's heart sank.

The chief walked towards her and wrapped her in his beefy arms before stepping back and sizing her up.

"I'm fine." She offered him a faint smile. "You can tell my father I am fine too."

"Oh now, Kat, you know he just worries. Iris has been worrying too. It took everything I had to convince her to stay at home and not come over here right away."

"I'll be sure to call her later."

"She'd appreciate that. Now, Detective O'Dell told me what happened. I want you to tell me your side now. Let's have a seat." He motioned towards the couch and Kat flashed a glance at Ian. He nodded briefly before leaving again with Travis. Sara sat in an adjacent chair and listened.

"Now start from the beginning. Detective O'Dell mentioned a brief encounter with Marshall Thompson at Giliano's..."

Kat exhaled and ran a hand through her hair, bits of glass filling her hand and she froze in the action so as not to scatter the pieces. "Okay. Well, we were waiting in line to order and Marshall walked up. Asked me if Travis relayed his message to me. I told him yes, but that I had no idea what he was talking about. I played it as if it meant nothing and went back to looking at the menu while also playing up Detective O'Dell as my boyfriend. Marshall finally got the hint and walked away. We then received our food and headed to the house."

"Did you notice anyone following you out of the restaurant? Any odd vehicles on your street?"

"No. Granted, I was not paying much attention. I was too busy focusing on... well I was rehashing everything that had just happened in the restaurant."

The chief nodded. "Okay, continue. You arrived at the house. What happened then?"

"We sat down and talked and ate our food. Then a bullet came through the window and shattered my lamp, and Ian pulled me to the floor and covered me. Multiple bullets started coming through and tearing through everything. Then that was it."

The chief added a note to his booklet and tucked it into his shirt pocket. "I'm glad you are safe, Kat, but this escalation in events troubles me. Even with police protection you are still being targeted. O'Dell has expressed concerns about the Chicago's Best Awards ceremony next week. He does not feel it is safe for you to attend."

"What?" Her head snapped up and her eyes narrowed. "When did he express that?"

"When he briefed me on the attack. The awards ceremony leaves you too exposed."

"No." Kat stood and began to pace back and forth once more. "Now more than ever I have to attend. These thugs have only attacked me when they cannot be seen. The odds of them barging into the ceremony with guns blazing is slim to none." She moved her hands as she spoke, her hands clenching into fists as she struggled to control her frustration.

The front door opened and Ian and Travis walked inside. Kat immediately barged towards Ian and pointed her finger in his chest. "You!" She poked him several times and he stood firmly with his hands by his side.

"I take it the chief told you my idea."

"Yes, and it is stupid. What happened to me wearing the necklace to draw Biggs and Marshall out?"

"That plan changed when you almost died tonight, Kat."

"No. No, no, no, no, no. I will be attending the ceremony whether the police department escorts me or not. If you do not wish to be my date anymore, then Jeremiah will go with me. Either way, I'm going. Necklace or no necklace."

"Think for a second, Kat. I told you from the beginning that if I felt your safety was compromised I would not allow this plan to happen. You can be upset with me, but the decision is final."

Kat looked to Travis and he avoided her gaze.

"So that's it? Our biggest opportunity to draw Biggs out and we are going to lose it because you're worried about me?" Her eyes shifted from one man to the next. "Is there nothing I can say to convince you?" She turned to the chief with imploring eyes. "I can do this, Albert. I know Detective O'Dell can keep me safe. Travis will keep me safe. I will be smart." She felt tears sting the back of her eyes as she pleaded for the chance to stop the madness that stemmed from Marshall Thompson. "Please Albert. This is our chance to put a stop to whatever Marshall has going on with Biggs. Let me help you."

"Kat, your father-"

"Would want me to help!" Kat exclaimed, throwing her hand in the air. "He wanted me to go into law enforcement in the first place. He would want me to do this. I will call him right now if I have to."

Chief Winters held up his hand to stop her. "No need, Kat. No need to bother your father this time of night. Give me the night to think it through. In the meantime, you get some rest. I've posted extra officers along the street and Starr and O'Dell will keep an eye on you here." He turned and nodded towards the two men as he walked to the door. When he left, Travis walked towards her. "We just worry, Kat. It's our job to keep you safe, and when we feel like we are not able to do that job, we have to make changes accordingly."

"I get it. I really do," she said in a huff. "But I'm not backing down on this. Even if another connection between Biggs and Marshall presented itself, I would still not be rid of Marshall. This is my chance to finally wash my hands of him. If I help bring him down, he will finally leave me alone." She shot a glance towards Ian as he slipped out of his shoes and kept silent.

"Okay," Travis agreed. "If the chief approves of the awards ceremony, I will not challenge his decision."

Hopeful, Kat hugged Travis tightly. "Thanks, Trav."

"Yeah, yeah, yeah, just don't make me regret it. And when O'Dell or I say to jump, duck, move, clap, sing, dance, or bolt, you listen to us."

"I will."

Travis cast a glance towards Ian and his partner stood stoically not revealing his thoughts on the matter. The doorbell rang and Ian and Travis both grabbed their weapons.

Kat held up her hands. "Whoa guys. I'm pretty sure drug lords don't ring doorbells."

"They might." Ian walked towards the front window and peeked through the curtains. He holstered his weapon. "It's Jeremiah."

Travis unlocked the door and Jeremiah hurried inside, his eyes wild with worry. When he spotted Kat, he walked up to her and immediately wrapped her in his arms. It was the true kindness of the gesture, the friend offering much needed comfort, that finally had her resolve melting and she allowed her nerves, frustrations, and tears to come. Jeremiah pulled back and cupped her face. "You okay, Kat? I came as soon as I heard. Sara texted me. You weren't hit, were you?" He lightly picked a piece of glass from her hair and looked at it in his fingers. He swiped his other hand over her face to absorb her tears. "I'm not hurt," she managed and slipped back into his embrace. "Thanks for coming to check on me."

"Of course. Always." Jeremiah nodded a greeting towards Travis and Ian. "So, what's the word?"

"Not sure who did it," Travis admitted. "We have extra patrols around the house tonight and O'Dell and I will be splitting shifts throughout the night to keep vigil.

"I'll help."

"No." Ian's voice was firm and had Jeremiah's back stiffen.

"Excuse me?"

"It has nothing to do with you, Jeremiah. You are not law enforcement that is the only reason I am saying no. Though your concern is appreciated, we will handle Kat's safety."

"Like you handled it tonight?!" Jeremiah yelled, his hand lightly stroking Kat's hair. "She could have been killed, O'Dell, and she was in your care."

Ian's jaw tightened, and his eyes forecasted a restrained storm. "You're right. I let my guard down. It will not happen again."

"What if I said that wasn't good enough?" Jeremiah challenged, darting a glance towards Travis.

"I completely understand that too." Ian continued. "I would just have to ask you to trust me."

"That's hard, considering." Jeremiah looked down at Kat. "I called your dad."

She backed away. "What? Why?"

"He would want to know about this latest incident, Kat." Jeremiah slid his hands into his pant pockets. "You can be mad at me if you want, but I'm not going to apologize."

"I'm not mad at you, Jer. I get it. I just... I was just hoping to keep him away from all of this."

"He beat me to it." Travis interjected. "I was going to call him in the morning."

"Wow, really? So all my big brothers think I need my daddy here to protect me?" She chuckled. "I guess I will always be a little girl when it comes to my dad. I want to be frustrated with you two for thinking I cannot handle this on my own, but I also appreciate the gesture. Because there is no one else I'd rather discuss this with than him. When will he be here?"

"He's taking the red eye, so first thing in the morning around five or so," Jeremiah answered. "I was going to swing by the airport to pick him up, but he assured me he could catch a cab."

"Good. I'll be curious to hear what he has to say once he's reviewed the case."

"We cannot share details of the case with a civilian, Kat." Ian reminded her.

Her jaw stiffened when she looked at him, her hands on her hips. "I assure you, Chief Winters will consult with my father on this case, Ian. He's participated in several cases in the past as well."

"It's not wise since you are his daughter. It is too personal."

"Okay, well then you can tell him that when he gets here. Until then, I suggest you plan on his help. I'm going to shower." She squeezed Jeremiah's hand before she walked towards the guestroom down the hall.

"Tread carefully, O'Dell." Travis warned quietly.

"You know as well as I do that nothing good could come from her father getting involved. The case would be too personal."

"I didn't mean with that. I meant with Kat," Travis clarified and then smirked as Ian stood dumbfounded. "I can tell there's a bit of a spark between you two. I would hate to see this case mess that up."

"For real," Sara interjected. "Talk about not taking the case personally. We all see the way you look at her, Ian."

Ian's mouth set in a firm line. "I see."

"We think it's great, though," Jeremiah chimed into the conversation, trying to ease some of the hostility he felt in the room.

"Well I guess on that note, I will catch some shut eye. You can take the first shift," Ian directed at Travis before he exited the room and shut the door to his bedroom.

"I hope he isn't upset with us," Sara whispered, lightly biting her lower lip in worry.

Travis lightly rubbed her back. "He'll get over it. It brought attention to his personal feelings being involved in the case and will hopefully convince him to be more open to the idea of Kat's dad helping us out. If anyone can, it's Dean Riesling." He kissed the top of her head. "Get some sleep. You staying?" He pointed towards Jeremiah and he shook his head. "Not unless you need me to. I was planning on it until O'Dell pointed out the extra patrols."

Travis nodded and walked Jeremiah to the front door, shaking his hand before he left. He slid the double lock into place and set the house alarm and sat comfortably in one of the overstuffed chairs of the living room to enjoy the quiet and keep his watch.

∞

Kat awoke to the sounds of muffled conversation drifting down the hallway. She turned to see that Sara had already departed the bedroom and lazily slung her legs over the side of the bed. Exhaustion wavered through her as she stood and stretched, the muscles in her back tight and finding slight reprieve. She quickly changed out of her sleep chemise into a snug pair of jeans and light cream sweater. Running a brush through her dark hair and fluffing it a bit with her fingers, she applied her make up. She was never one to wear many cosmetics, so she kept it light, but she did apply a faint coat of lipstick. She chalked her extra effort up to the fact that her father was coming into town, but truth made her mind wander to Ian. She added a light touch of perfume and then made her way down the hall towards the warm, open kitchen and living space. She spotted her father's salt and pepper hair leaning over several files spread out on the coffee table as he and Ian talked in hushed tones. She nodded a greeting to Travis and Sara in the kitchen as she made her way to the two men.

"I hate to interrupt this powwow, but I find myself in need of one of the best hugs from Tennessee." She watched as her dad's head snapped up and a wide smile flashed her way. He stood and caught her as she ran forward and jumped into his arms. He swung her around and set her on her feet, his hands resting upon her shoulders and his pensive gaze surveying her. "I'm fine, Dad," she admitted before he could ask.

"I can see that now. Though Detective O'Dell assured me of that fact, I must say it was hard to let you continue sleeping when I wanted to barge into your room and check on you. How are you doing mentally, Squirt?"

"Good. Annoyed, but good." She offered a smile before her eyes travelled towards Ian. "Morning."

"Morning, Kat," he greeted, as he stood to his feet. She walked towards him and slipped an arm around his waist as she faced her father. "Did Detective O'Dell inform you that he is my fake boyfriend?"

Her father chuckled. "He did." With a knowing gaze, her father winked at Ian before giving his daughter a reassuring smile. "And have you been a sweet girlfriend?"

"Of course I have." She slapped a hand on Ian's chest with a little more force than necessary making him slightly flinch. She looked up at him with a smug grin. "He's the luckiest man on the force."

Laughing heartily, Dean Riesling nodded. "Of that I have no doubt. Any man would be lucky to have my beautiful daughter on his arm."

Kat rolled her eyes as she looked up at Ian with a small smirk. His eyes were serious and had her face sobering as she felt his hand lift to brush her hair behind her ear. The gesture was tender, intimate, and far too enjoyable and she started to pull away, but his arm tightened around her shoulders. It was then she noticed the bandage on the back of his hand. "What happened?" She pulled his hand towards her and brushed her fingers over the white medical tape.

"Just a scratch," Ian assured her.

"That's a serious bandage for just a scratch," she replied, lifting his hand to see if she could find some fault in the bandage to check the severity of his injury.

"A piece of glass must have snagged me last night during the shooting. Nothing serious. I'll be fine." He held her gaze once more and her father watched with an interested expression. He shot Travis a look of curiosity and saw the light lift to the young man's brows as if warning him his daughter's affections were more genuine for Detective O'Dell than just pretending. And if the tenderness expressed by the stoic detective was any indication, his affections towards Kat were more than a show.

"Detective O'Dell filled me in on last night's events in more detail." Dean stepped forward and sat back in his seat as he waved his hand over the files on the table. "It seems Marshall has his hand in with some heavy hitters, Kat. Have you talked to him about it?"

"What?" She strayed her eyes away from Ian to stare at her father. "Why would I talk to Marshall about anything?"

"I'm just asking, my dear."

"Well the answer is no. I have tried to keep Marshall Thompson out of my life, thank you very much."

"Good. As a father, I am glad to hear that. As an officer of the law, I'm trying to dig deeper into why you are connected to all this if connections with Marshall have been severed."

"You doubt me?" she asked. Annoyance laced her voice as she crossed her arms and eased into a chair.

Ian lightly brushed a hand over her hair before he sat on the armrest next to her. "He's not accusing you, Kat. All bases have to be covered. Even the most insignificant contact with Marshall could have stirred him to make some sort of decision or plan."

"The only contact I have had with the man in the past year has been in passing. I've ignored him, and he never said anything. It wasn't until the bust in the alley that he actually started talking to me again or showing up. And you have been with me during all of those meetings." She motioned towards Ian before running her hands through her hair. Ian reached down and grabbed one of her hands and threaded his fingers with hers. Resting their joined hands on his knee, he looked to the former chief. "Sir, we have been over all the angles with Kat. The only thing that ties her to Marshall is the diamond necklace. Our plan for the Chicago's Best Awards is the best shot we have at establishing the true connection between Marshall and Biggs."

Dean Riesling briefly glanced at their joined hands. Saying nothing, he nodded. "I know. That's the only link I can find as well. It seems my help isn't much needed."

"Don't look so disappointed, Dad." Kat grinned. "You're always needed." She rose and walked over and sat beside him and rested her head on his shoulder. He patted her knee. "You are too much like your mother sometimes, Squirt. It makes my heart smile."

She kissed him loudly on the cheek before standing. "I think I am going to eat some breakfast now. Have you two had anything other than coffee this morning?" she asked.

The two men shook their heads.

"I figured. Maybe we could all go to the café for breakfast. It will give me a chance to check on things, give you a chance to see the place and how much it's grown." She waved towards her dad. "And give you a chance to play your part of my boyfriend even better by showing up with my dad." She motioned towards Ian. "Nothing says serious relationship like hanging out with my dad." Dean's smile faltered a bit, and Ian noticed the former chief did not quite like the idea of a false relationship with his daughter.

"Whatever you would like to do, Kat." Ian slid his hands into his pockets to prevent reaching out to her.

She clapped her hands. "Then it's settled. Come on Dad. You can ride with us." She walked towards the door, grabbing her purse from the side table, her father following behind her. "We'll see you two later." She waved towards Travis and Sara as she linked her arm with Ian's.

«CHAPTER TEN»

"MY GOODNESS, SQUIRT, this place looks incredible." Dean turned a small circle as he took in the bustling café and the long line of customers waiting to order. "I see Jeremiah is still working out."

"He is. Best employee I could ever ask for." Kat waved at Jeremiah as he looked up to greet them.

"He's a good man, I am glad you took a chance on him." Dean turned towards Ian. "You know the story of Jeremiah and Kat?" he asked.

"Yes sir." He smiled and lightly tugged Kat's hair as she rolled her eyes.

"It's not a secret, Dad," she added before walking towards an open booth.

"Ah, but it is not common knowledge. I bet you didn't even tell Ian. I bet he found out himself, am I right?"

"Jeremiah told me," Ian replied, noting Kat's surprise.

Jeremiah walked up and shook Dean's hand. "Good to see you again, sir. Ian," he greeted.

"I want my usual, Jer," Kat stated. She waved her hand towards her dad. "What about you, Dad?"

"I'll have the breakfast special."

"Ian?" Jeremiah asked.

"Coffee for me, thanks."

"You need more than coffee." Kat turned towards Jeremiah. "Blueberry muffin for the detective."

"You got it." Jeremiah hustled off and Kat turned back to face her father. Ian's cell phone rang and he glanced at the caller id. "My apologies, but I need to take this." He slid out of the booth leaving an emptiness next to her that washed Kat in disappointment.

"You like him." Her father pointed out.

Kat focused her attention away from a pacing Ian and back to her father. "What?"

He grinned. "I said, you like him."

She felt her face blush before trying to tamper it down. "What makes you say that?"

"I see the way you two interact, and it is not just for show." Dean lightly tapped the side of his nose. "I have a sense about these things."

Kat crossed her arms in amusement. "Oh really? Let's say I am somewhat interested in Ian. Would he receive the Dad seal of approval?"

"I think so." Dean watched the younger man as he continued his conversation and periodically glanced in Kat's direction to keep an eye on her. "I still do not know enough about him, but I like what I see. He also seems to care about you, which I find to be a good thing. It means he will try harder in keeping you safe."

"You think he cares about me? What makes you think that?"

"I wasn't born yesterday, Squirt. I know when a man is interested in a woman."

She flushed again and her dad waved away their conversation as Ian approached and slid back into the booth beside Kat.

"Everything okay?" she asked.

"Sorry about that. Yes, everything seems to be fine. That was Travis just looping me in on the morning meeting with the Chief."

"You didn't have to be there?" Kat asked.

"My job is to protect you." He lightly tapped the tip of her nose before turning to receive his order from Jeremiah. The blueberry muffin made his mouth water, and he inwardly thanked Kat for ordering it for him.

"Am I to have you following me around all day?" Kat took a sip of her coffee as she studied him over the brim.

"For most of it."

"But I am supposed to go shopping with Sara today to pick out a dress for the award ceremony."

"That's fine." He took a sip of his drink.

"Um, no, it is not," Kat countered, "you cannot see my dress before the big night."

"I did not realize it was to be a secret."

Dean laughed and shook his head. "Son, you have a lot to learn about women."

Ian looked confused and Kat slid her arm through his and leaned her head against his shoulder. "My dad will go with us so that I am safely guarded and you can take care of stuff at the station for a bit. Then we can meet up afterwards and you may resume guard duties."

Ian looked to her dad and Mr. Riesling nodded. "I can keep an eye on the girls for a bit today. It will give you time to go over things with Travis and the Chief."

Ian looked unsure, and Kat lightly kissed his cheek. He turned to her, surprise in his green eyes as she lowered her voice. "I will be fine, Ian. You don't have to worry about me with my dad here."

Sighing, he draped his arm over the back of the booth and leaned towards her, his lips a breath away from her ear. Whispering, his breath rustled her hair and made her skin hum. "I am your boyfriend, it is my job to worry." He pulled back slightly so their eyes met, and Kat found herself drawn to him.

"I think I will go catch up with Jeremiah while things are slow and leave you two to talk this out." Dean retreated quickly so as not to interrupt the intimate conversation and moment between Ian and his daughter. Kat shook away the moment and watched her dad hastily move out of the booth. "Dad-" Her words trailed off as she watched him continue walking towards the front of the café. She felt Ian's finger on her jaw as he turned her face back towards his. "Where all do you plan on going to dress shop?"

"Why?"

"I need an idea, just in case something comes up and I need to get there quickly."

"How about I text you each time I go into a different store so that you know where I am at all times? Would that be better?"

"Yes, that would work."

"So you're going to let me escape for a bit?"

"Escape? Am I smothering you?" He eased back with a baffled expression on his face, and what she sensed as hurt.

"What? No. I didn't mean it like that. I meant escape the police protection, not you."

"I am the protection detail." His voice carried a tone of frustration as she slid closer to him. His hand absentmindedly went to her hair as she faced him.

"I didn't mean it like that, Ian. I love having you around, truly. I just meant that it will be nice to get my mind off of this whole Marshall business. And unfortunately, you are part of that too. So sometimes it feels like-"

"All work, no play," he finished.

"Exactly. I just need a breather from the charade."

"I get it, Kat. I do."

"You aren't upset with me?"

His finger lightly brushed her cheek. "No, I am not upset."

"Good." She kissed him softly on the cheek. "On the bright side, you will get to see me in a beautiful new dress." She winked as he laughed.

"And of that, I am truly grateful." He grabbed her hand and kissed her fingers. "What time did you plan to ditch me?"

She groaned playfully and nudged him. "I'm thinking right now if you keep that up, O'Dell."

Laughing, he slid from the booth and extended his hand towards her, helping her from the booth. Her father walked up. "Well did you two decide on a plan?"

"Yes." Kat slid her arm around Ian's waist and he tugged her close into his side, his hand rubbing her arm before settling around her shoulders. "Ian is going to the station now, and you and I will grab Sara and start shopping. Aren't you excited, Dad?"

"Very," he said, his false amusement making them all laugh.

Ian squeezed Kat's shoulders once more and released her. "Alright then, you two have fun today, and," he held up his cell phone, "keep me updated. I will see you sometime this afternoon." He stepped to walk towards the door and Kat grabbed his hand.

"Whoa there, mister," she pulled him back towards her, her free hand grabbing the front of his shirt. She kissed him hard on the lips before releasing him. "Now you may go."

Ian felt the air leave his lungs and his pulse skyrocket. Kat continually surprised him and left him breathless. He felt the heat color his neck as her father's scrutiny weighed upon him. He squeezed her hand one more time and walked out of the café, his mind reeling with the feelings Kat's kiss brought forth and the impact it had on his heart.

∞

Ian ran his hands through his hair and tugged as Travis tossed out yet another unsatisfying plan.

"I can tell you don't like that idea," Travis eased onto a stool in front of the large whiteboard and studied their case notes. "Okay, so let's say we send Kat in with the necklace on right here," he marked a spot on the banquet hall layout, "that puts her right near the entrance to her table. Now, the banquet plans show Marshall's table over here across the room." He marked another spot on the map and rubbed his chin. "She would be clearly visible. Plus, he is more than likely going to be watching for her arrival anyway."

"And what do we do if Marshall is not already seated?" Ian asked.

"Sara and I will already be inside. I'll give you the all clear. Simple."

Ian's grim expression had Travis rolling his eyes. "Come on, O'Dell. I know you are not going to like any of the plans we come up with, but you have to admit this makes the most sense. We need Marshall to first see the necklace at a distance. Give him time to ponder and to panic. This is the best way."

Sighing, Ian leaned forward, his elbows on his knees. "You're right, I don't like it. I don't like the idea of Kat going to this event at all. But since I am outnumbered, I'm trying to be cooperative. But we are fools if we think Biggs is going to show up to this gig."

"He's not." Travis confirmed. "But after spotting the necklace, the people Marshall interacts with will give us more people to look into, and that might be the lead we need." Pleased with himself, Travis leaned back against the wall and crossed his arms. "So," he grinned, "what kind of dress do you think Kat will wear?"

Ian blinked and shook his head turning to face Travis. "What does it matter?"

"Oh come on, O'Dell! You're killing me!" Travis hopped to his feet and slapped Ian on the shoulder as he walked towards his desk. "We all see the way you two interact. Your little 'false' romance has turned into something else." Travis held up his finger to deter the argument he saw coming from Ian. "Don't deny it," he ordered. "Kat pulls out all the stops for this event. Every year she and Sara buy elaborate dresses, have their hair done, their make up done, etc. She's going to look good."

"Okay." Ian wasn't quite sure how he was to respond, though he could not deny he was eager to see the transformation. Kat was beautiful already, but he would be lying to himself if he did not admit he could not wait to see her in her finest.

"Okay?" Travis shook his head in dismay. "You are the worst man I have ever met. Aren't you at least a little curious?"

"I am. Doesn't mean I have to become a drooling fool about it." He tossed Travis his keys, knowing full well that was what his partner was searching for on his messy desk.

"Whatever. If you ask me, you could be a drooling fool for once. Loosen up a bit. You coming?" Travis waited at the door. Ian grabbed his wallet and followed.

Making their way through the precinct, Travis nodded greetings to friends and fellow officers as Ian silently followed, lost in his own thoughts. *Would he be able to keep Kat safe?* That was the thought plaguing him and leaving him unsettled. Travis was right, Ian's feelings for Kat had transformed from pretend to reality, and the thought of him failing her tied his stomach into knots and made his jaw clench. *If he had two minutes alone with Marshall Thompson, the damage he could do...* His thought trailed off as a black sedan pulled into the station parking lot, as he and Travis were about to hop into Travis' truck. Marshall Thompson stepped out and angrily made his way towards them. Several officers leaving for their lunch breaks paused to watch the confrontation.

"You have no right!" Marshall bellowed, as he pointed a finger at Travis, his sharp gaze flashing towards Travis and then to Ian.

"Marshall," Travis greeted stoically. "To what do we owe the pleasure?"

"I've seen your police surveillance on me. You have no right, no warrant, and absolutely no authority to allow such a thing. I have done nothing to warrant a tail."

"We have no idea what you are talking about," Ian stated, slipping on his sunglasses as if bored with the conversation.

Marshall scoffed. "Please! The black SUVs are pretty recognizable. Look, Detective, if you do not want me to speak to your 'girlfriend,' then maybe you should tell her to stop playing games and give me what I want."

"If she had any idea what that would be, I'm sure she would." Ian countered. "But considering she has no idea what you are talking about, and you won't tell her, then I think you are wasting all of our time. Ready?" He turned his attention to Travis and Travis nodded, unlocking the doors to his truck.

"I am the most powerful attorney in this city. Do not think I will not take this matter to the district attorney's office. We'll see how smug you are after that," Marshall threatened.

Travis offered a small wave as they backed out and headed towards the café for lunch. "I'm so over him," Travis muttered.

"What tail was he talking about?" Ian asked. Confused, he dialed the chief's number. "Hey Chief. Question: We don't have a police tail on Thompson, do we?" He waited patiently as he listened. "Roger that. Just making sure. Thompson just rolled up to the precinct accusing Starr and me of having him followed. Black SUVs, he says. Must be Biggs. Might want to have a tail on him now just to see who is really following him." Ian wrapped up his conversation with the chief and glanced at his text messages. "Where is Giselle's?"

"Giselle's?" Travis repeated with a wide smile. "It's only the swankiest dress shop over on Fifth. Is that where the girls are at?"

"Yeah, Kat just texted."

"Man, she wasn't kidding when she said she was going to get the best dress. She's not afraid to spend the department's money." Travis laughed.

"Should we swing by there?"

"No. Dean's looking out for them today. We are meant to be planning the award's night. Stop trying to finagle a way to go see Kat."

"I'm not. I just…" Ian ran a hand over his stubbled jaw, "it's hard to trust someone else with her safety right now."

"Even her own dad?" Travis asked in bewilderment. "You do realize he was the police chief for over thirty years, don't you?"

"I'm well aware," Ian grumbled as he sent a text back to Kat.

∞

"He's asking me to send him pictures of possible choices." Kat grinned at Sara as they sat in the dressing room and Sara twirled around in a slinky black dress.

"No way," Sara demanded. "It is a surprise. Tell him that."

Kat stifled a laugh as she sent back a message. Her smile widened at his response.

"You two are seriously crushing on one another. Why don't you guys just make your relationship official? The real deal."

"What?" Kat looked up and her smile vanished. "We can't. This is just for this case. Besides, whether I like him or not, I'm in no place to have a relationship right now."

"Why not?"

"Because I'm busy." Even to her own ears, Kat's answer fell flat.

"Seriously?" Sara laughed as she stepped out of the dressing room and Kat's father sat on a white sofa. "What do you think, Mr. Riesling?"

"Very beautiful, Sara. Travis' heart will surely stop."

Her answering smile had him chuckling as he waited to see what Kat chose to try.

"Oh, she's not in a dress." Sara motioned over her shoulder as Kat stepped out, pushing the changing curtain aside. "They are at the café eating lunch. Maybe we should go." Her voice held hope and her eyes narrowed as she saw both Sara and her dad shaking their heads. "Why not?"

"You are to be buying a dress and he is to be working," Sara pointed out. "They're both pathetic. You would think they would wise up already and admit they want to be together."

"Hey now," Kat interrupted, "I just wanted to see where they are at with their plans."

"Liar." Sara and Dean replied in unison. Kat's lips twitched as she fought down the smile.

"Fine. I will just tell Ian you two are holding me hostage then."

"I wouldn't tell him that," Sara teased, "knowing Ian he would come in here guns blazing trying to rescue you."

Kat grinned. "One could only hope." She wriggled her eyebrows as her dad laughed and Sara rolled her eyes.

"Come on, you hopeless romantic, we need to go find you a dress now. I'll go change really quick." Sara swept her way back into the dressing room as Kat sat beside her father.

He lightly squeezed her knee. "You didn't see any dresses you liked, Squirt?"

She shrugged. "Not yet. I keep waiting for that 'Aha!' moment, but haven't had it yet. Hopefully the next shop will have something." She glanced at her phone again hoping for another text.

"He's probably eating, dear." Her father winked at her as she blushed.

"I was just checking the time."

"I see." Dean pulled her into a side hug. "It pleases me to see you interested in someone. Are you sure Detective O'Dell is worth it?"

"What do you mean? Do you not like him? I thought you said you did?" Kat's voice held worry as she looked into her father's face. A face she loved and had missed more than she could express. He lightly kissed her forehead. "I think he is a nice man, what little I know of him. I just want to make sure he is the right man to have my daughter's affections."

"You doubt him?"

"It's a bit early for me to make that call," Dean answered honestly. "He seems rather taken with you, but he currently has a part to play. Though I sense some genuine feelings on his part, as well as yours', my verdict is still out."

Kat's shoulders slumped.

"Don't look disappointed, Squirt. I like him. He seems like a great man. It is just hard to think of any man being worthy of my only daughter." He lightly tugged on her hair as her faced eased into a smile.

"Thanks, Dad. I like Ian, I honestly do, but I'm like you. My verdict is still out. Who's to say our emotions are not just getting tangled up in the moment? I want to wait and see how we are after this investigation ends. That will be the true test."

"Smart girl."

"But is it wrong of me to still want to knock his socks off at the award's ceremony?"

"Not at all." Dean winked at her as she looked up as Sara walked out of the dressing room carrying her dress of choice.

"Is that the one?" Dean asked, nodding towards the black gown.

Sara beamed. "It is. Travis won't know what to do with himself when he sees me in this."

Dean laughed and gestured them towards the register. "We should move along then and find your dress now, Squirt."

∞

Kat turned and surveyed her reflection in the pearl-colored gown. The silk clung to her slight frame and showcased what little curves she possessed, while the low back added a seductive appeal while remaining tasteful. She stepped out of the dressing room and Sara gasped. "Kat! That is beautiful!"

Kat slowly turned so that Sara and her dad could study her. "You think so? Dad?"

"It is beautiful, sweetheart, absolutely beautiful." Kat smiled as she nodded towards the mirror and slowly slid her hands down the front of the dress to smooth out imaginary wrinkles. The soft and sensuous fabric felt smooth under her fingers. "Yes, I think this is the dress." She looked to Sara and without having to ask her question her friend popped to her feet and clapped her hands. "And Ian is going to die." Sara stated.

"Well that wouldn't be good." Kat laughed.

"Die in a good way, as in his head will explode, or he'll have a heart attack because you've stopped his heart with your beauty." Sara waved her hand as she continued describing different ways Kat would shock Ian.

"Okay, okay, okay, we get it." Kat exhaled deeply as she studied her reflection one more time before turning back towards the dressing room. "After this I wanted to head to the craft shop across the street," she called over her shoulder.

"Why?" Sara asked, her voice drifting over the curtains.

"Ian said his mom worked at a craft store because she loves to knit, so I thought I would try to find a beginners' book. I think it might be fun to try and learn." Kat's comment had Sara and Dean sharing a knowing look before she stepped out of the dressing room, her dress draped over her arm. "Do you guys mind?"

"Not at all," they answered.

"Good. Let me go pay for this and then we can head over there."

"Is it the store his mother works at?" Sara asked, trailing behind her.

"I'm not sure. He didn't tell me. Why?"

"Just curious," Sara answered.

Kat paid for the dress and waited patiently as the cashier slipped it into a long plastic bag, tying off the bottom so the dress would not drag. She handed the clothes hanger to Kat and waved them away with a smile. As they waited at the crosswalk, Kat surveyed the crowd. She didn't often venture to this side of city, and her mind worked on ways she could possibly cater to a bigger market. The crosswalk countdown began as they headed towards the small craft store on the corner.

"The Crafty Corner. Hmmm... clever," Sara admitted, noting the location.

Kat giggled as she opened the door, the old, creaking brass hinges giving away their entrance.

"Welcome," a voice greeted from behind a row of patterns. A short older woman stepped out and smiled. "Is there something I may help you find?"

Kat handed her dress to her father as she stepped forward. "Actually, yes. I am hoping to learn how to knit and was wondering if there was a guide book of some kind."

The woman's face brightened as she nodded. "Oh yes, follow me." As Kat disappeared with the worker, Sara lightly fingered the different ribbons while Dean stood towards the entrance, his eyes on the street. He squinted as a black sedan slowly drove passed. He checked his watch to monitor the time and kept his eyes glued to the street. Five minutes later, the same car passed by again.

"Sara, dear?"

"Yes sir?" She glanced up.

"Would you mind texting Travis our location. I didn't see Kat forward that information to Ian when we arrived."

"Sure."

"Or better yet, do you have Ian's phone number?"

"No, sorry, but I can give you Travis'."

He waited as she spouted off a phone number. He dialed it quickly and held the phone up to his ear. Travis answered on the first ring.

"I need to speak to Ian." Dean's voice was low as he ordered Travis to hand his phone over.

"O'Dell." The younger man's voice carried over the line just as Dean saw the black sedan pass by again.

"We have a problem." Dean paused as Kat walked towards the checkout, right in line with the windows. "You need to get here now. Black sedan has passed by every five minutes, 3 times, and has now parked along the curb. I think we are being watched."

"We're on our way. We're just a couple of blocks over. Three minutes, Mr. Riesling." Ian hung up and ordered Travis to turn down the next side street. "Park in the back. I don't want these guys to see us enter the building."

They arrived in five minutes thanks to the heavy traffic, and Ian felt an eerie sense of unease as he hurried towards the back entrance. When he opened the door, he heard screams and quickly he and Travis made their way towards the front of the shop. Ian's gaze spotted his mother hunkered down behind the counter, her eyes wide, but alert. She stood slowly upon seeing him. "You okay?" He asked. She nodded and accepted a quick hug from him as his gaze travelled to the floor where Kat huddled over her father, her hands pressed to his side. She glanced up, a quick relief flashed in her eyes before she focused again on her dad. Travis shouted into his cell phone for back up and an ambulance as Ian evaluated Dean's injury.

"He was shot." Kat's voice quivered as she sniffled back the tears that streaked her face. Her hands were covered in blood as she continued applying pressure to her father's wound. Ian gently touched her hands. "Looks like it was a through and through. No major arteries or internal organs hit. Just keep applying pressure, Kat. I'm going to find something to use to help." He stood up and reached for the first bolt of fabric he saw, quickly unwinding several yards and tearing it. He wadded it up and pressed it hard against Dean's side as the older man groaned. Kat leaned over him, "Daddy, you're going to be okay. Just hang in there. The ambulance is on the way. Okay?"

Dean's eyes blinked back the pain and he found Ian's steady gaze as he now applied pressure to his wound. "Three men in the sedan. The plates are written on my palm." He lifted his hand and Ian memorized the letters and numbers.

"Daddy," Kat continued, "just a little bit longer." Her voice dropped to a whisper. "Why is there so much blood?" She looked to Ian in a panic and he glanced up at his mother. The older woman rounded the counter and knelt beside Kat, pulling her into a side hug. "Oh sweetie, your father is going to be just fine. He seems to be a tough man, and the ambulance is almost here." She lightly brushed aside Kat's hair with motherly affection. "Now, now, now, you just sit right here." She eased Kat into a sitting position on the floor leaning against the cash counter. She noticed Kat's hands shaking and took them into her own. Kat looked up and caught the woman's warm gaze. She then looked to Ian. "Y-you're his mother." She commented.

The woman smiled, her face lighting up as she nodded sweetly. "Yes, dear, I am. Now why don't we just take some of this fabric and wipe your hands off?" She tore a large piece of fabric and placed it over Kat's hands and began to rub away the blood. Sirens tore through the air as Chief Winters and several other officers stormed into the shop followed by the EMT crew. Her father was loaded onto a stretcher and Kat bolted to her feet to follow them to the ambulance. Chief Winters caught her arm. "I will go with him, Kat. O'Dell is to take you home. Now. I will let you know when it is safe to come to the hospital."

"But-"

The chief shook his head and turned to hop into the back of the ambulance. Kat stood, shoulders slumped as she watched her dad being carried away to the hospital. "I have to call my mom." She reached into her pocket for her phone but it wasn't there. She couldn't remember where it was, and her hands shook as she began trying to dig in her purse to find it. Ian gingerly took hold of her purse strap and gently tugged it out of her hands and placed it on the counter top. Kat's hands dropped to her sides before she started fumbling with the bloodied fabric on the floor. He took that from her hands as well.

"Ian, please." Her words trailed off as tears poured down her cheeks. He pulled her to him in a tight embrace, his hands smoothing her hair as she sobbed into his chest. His mother walked forward and lightly placed her hand on Kat's back as they both waited for her fear and nerves to subside. When she had finally gathered herself together, Kat swiped her hands over her face and looked up at Ian. "I need to get to the hospital."

"No, Kat, I'm taking you home. Chief's orders."

"But I need to be there with my dad, Ian." Her eyes implored him and though he wished he could give her what she wanted, he stood firm.

"I'm sorry, but you would just be placing him in even more danger by being there right now. Is there someone you could call?"

A light flashed in her eyes and she nodded. "Yes. Yes, I can call Jeremiah." She glanced around, trying again to figure out where she had placed her phone. Ian handed her his and she dialed. "Jer, hey it's Kat." She took a step away from Ian and his mother as she continued her conversation.

"She's lovely." His mother whispered.

Ian looked down at his mother and shook his head. "It's not what you think, Mom."

She innocently held up her hands. "I didn't say a word."

"But I see you thinking it," Ian muttered as Kat walked up. "He's headed over there now. I told him to find the chief and make sure he had Albert tell the staff he was to be treated as family to my dad so they could keep him updated."

"Good. Jeremiah was a great choice."

"I just need to make a couple of phone calls to the café later to make sure Anna can handle things while we are both out. She should be able to, but it's been a while since she's had to manage on her own." She talked fast, her nerves making her voice unstable, and she wound her hands around his phone in a death grip as if waiting for a call at any moment.

"Let's get you out of here." Ian placed his hand at the small of her back and began leading her towards the back of the store. She stopped quickly and had him bumping into her. "Is something wrong?"

"Your mom. Do we not need to stay and help her with this?" She motioned towards the destruction that consumed the small shop.

"No. I called my dad earlier and he is on the way, plus Travis is not leaving until all the evidence is collected. Mainly bullet casings. This is a crime scene now, Kat. It will be awhile before she can leave. She needs to give her statement."

"Did you want to wait until your dad arrives?" Though he did not admit it, she could tell he was worried about his mother too. She hated to take him away from his family after such an event.

"He'll be here any moment. We need to leave. Now." He redirected her towards the back door and towards Travis' truck. "My dad will keep me updated."

Kat slid into the passenger seat, her eyes darting to the alleyway and any suspicious shadows or persons, but nothing seemed out of the ordinary. Ian's cell phone rang and Kat quickly relinquished her hold and answered in a hurried tone. "Hello?" She paused. "Oh, yes, of course." She handed the phone to Ian and mouthed 'sorry.'

"O'Dell."

She strained to listen, but found her eyes growing heavy. Whatever adrenaline had kept her going was quickly fading and before she knew it, she fell asleep.

«CHAPTER ELEVEN»

KAT AWOKE IN TRAVIS' guestroom with a light blanket draped over her as she lay in the same clothes she had on from her shopping trip with Sara. She rose up to her elbows and immediately regretted the move. Her entire body ached. With a slight moan, she rolled off the bed to her feet and made her way to the shower. She felt gritty and the glass in her hair needed to be removed, as well as her father's blood that still stained her hands. She wasn't sure how long she had been asleep, and though she was sore, she felt somewhat better. Her stomach growled and she made a mental note to stop in the kitchen after her shower. She never did eat lunch, she realized, and as she stepped into the steaming shower, she felt some of her concerns melt away with the hot water. She made a mental list of what she needed to accomplish once she emerged from the glorious spray. First was food, while also phoning Jeremiah to receive an update on her dad. Then it was phoning Anna to make sure the café was running smoothly. After that, she would focus on Ian and what had happened earlier. She scrubbed her hands, the blood pooling around the drain as the water erased the horrific events of the day. *Her poor dad.* He had only come to help and he ended up being wounded. And it was her fault. If she had just given Marshall the necklace to begin with, none of this would have happened. Reprimanding herself, Kat stepped out of the shower and made haste in slipping into fresh clothes. Hair still wet, she shuffled down the hallway to the kitchen. Surprise crossed her face when she saw her mom sitting with Ian's mother in the living room, Travis and Ian sat at the dining table with a man Kat had never seen before, and Sara stood in the kitchen mixing something in a large glass bowl.

"Hey you," Sara greeted. "How are you feeling?"

"I feel better, but I feel like I've been run over by a semi."

"You look better, anyway," Sara noted as she poured her concoction into a baking dish.

"What are you making?"

"I'm making that spaghetti dish you taught me. It's almost time for dinner and we both know how terrible I am in the kitchen, but look," she held up her phone with a picture of Kat's recipe card, "I saved this and have followed it to the letter. So it should turn out okay."

A small smile tilted Kat's lips at her friend's accomplishment. "Good job. I'm sure it will be delicious. I could honestly eat a horse right about now." She fished through the refrigerator and emerged with a cheese stick. "But this will tide me over. Need any help?"

"Nope. I'm just going to toast some garlic bread and toss together a salad. You go relax. Your mom arrived about an hour ago." She motioned towards the living room.

"I see that." She walked towards the living room. "Mom?"

Renee Riesling looked up and her eyes flooded with concern and a mother's worry. "Oh baby," she whispered as she bolted to her feet and swept Kat into a tight hug. "I'm so sorry about all of this. Your daddy is doing fine. He made it out of surgery about an hour and a half ago. Jeremiah is staying with him right now." She smoothed her hand over Kat's damp hair and eased her down onto the couch beside her. "Mrs. O'Dell and I were just talking."

Kat found Ian's mother's gaze and tried to offer a smile, but she felt emotionally raw and felt tears burning the back of her eyes. "She brought your dress over." Renee motioned towards the bagged dress draped over one of the spare chairs.

"Thank you."

"You're very welcome, dear." She smiled warmly. "Thankfully it was not ruined in today's commotion."

"That is good, though I doubt I will be given the opportunity to wear it now."

"I wouldn't say that." Ian walked up and leaned over the back of the couch, lightly kissing the top of her head. She leaned back and looked up at him. "What?"

He smiled and rounded the furniture sitting on the coffee table across from her. He gently grabbed her hands. "Good to see you awake and hopefully somewhat refreshed."

"Yeah, I'm sorry about that. Last thing I remember is being in the car. Thanks for bringing me in."

"You're welcome." His thumb brushed her knuckles.

Their two mothers watched as their children conversed. Knowing glances had them exchanging small smiles as they silently slipped away to give them privacy.

"Starr and I have continued mapping out a plan for the award's night. If you are willing, we think it is now a great idea that you are there. Though it will be even more dangerous than originally planned."

"I'm in."

He chuckled. "Don't you want to hear the rest of the plan?"

"I don't have to, I trust you, and I will do whatever I have to do to bring Marshall and Biggs to justice."

He lightly brushed her cheek with his hand. "Slow down, tiger."

She smirked.

"The danger has escalated to a point we should not even be considering taking you to the award's ceremony."

"But you are."

"Yes."

"Why?" she asked.

"Because the brazen attempt today tells us that either Biggs or Marshall is getting desperate. They want the necklace."

"Assuming it is the necklace they are after," Kat added.

"Yes."

"What I don't understand is why they keep attacking me. Obviously they know by now that I don't carry it in my pocket. What's the point in going after me at this point? By now, Biggs should know I have nothing to do with Marshall, and Marshall should know that I want nothing to do with him. I don't understand."

"Perhaps both men think you know more than you do."

"I guess, but to try and kill me? That seems a bit extreme."

"You would be surprised, Kat. People will do crazy things to tie up loose ends." He squeezed her hands as she sighed and leaned back against the cushions.

"This is all so insane. Just the other day I was a happy café owner feeding my cats, and today I'm one kill shot away from being... well... killed. And what? All for a stupid necklace that's been hiding in my pantry for over a year. It just seems silly and ridiculous."

"Hey." He tapped her chin with his finger. "It will all be over soon and your life will return back to normal. Gato, Chat, and Kissa are doing fine, and you will be back to the café and back to your old life before you know it."

She sighed and lightly closed her eyes. "What I wouldn't give for an all-nighter making bread."

He laughed. "I was thinking more along the lines of those cookies."

Grinning, she raised his hand to her cheek and briefly rested against it. "After helping me rid my life of Marshall Thompson, you can have free cookies for life."

"Wow." His brows rose. "Really? Maybe I should have mentioned more of your treats."

Playfully she swatted him. "Don't get crazy, Detective O'Dell."

As he smiled, the doorbell rang and all good feelings vanished from his face as he switched into 'detective mode.' Travis and Ian slinked towards the door, weapons drawn. Travis peeked out of the side curtain and then relaxed. "Flower delivery guy."

"Flowers?" Sara asked, disappointment on her face. "What company?"

Travis peeked again. "Robert's Roses."

Sara wrinkled her nose.

"Real place?" Ian asked her.

She nodded. "My competition."

Ian nodded for Travis to open the door while he stood to the side, his weapon still at the ready should the delivery be a set up.

"I have a delivery for a Kat Riesling," the young man reported, handing the flower bouquet to Travis and accepting his signature. "Have a rosy day," the man deadpanned with no enthusiasm as he trudged back to the beat up van parked along the curb. Ian relaxed as Travis walked the flowers over to Kat. "For you."

Her brow furrowed as she slipped the small card from the plastic stand. "More carnations. I think I know who these are from."

"Who?" both men asked.

"The same person who sent me the purple ones. My secret admirer." She read the card and nodded. "Yep. Same person."

Ian snatched the card from her fingers. "Still no idea who that could be."

"Nope." Kat shrugged and leaned back against the cushions again. Suddenly, she bolted up into a sitting position. "Check them."

"What?" Travis asked, confused.

Katharine E. Hamilton

"Check them for a bug."

"Why would they be bugged?" Travis asked her.

"Because the night Ian and I were at my house no one knew and yet someone came and shot up the place. The only way they would have known is if a bug had been planted. I had the flowers on my fireplace mantle."

Ian grabbed the bouquet and began removing the flowers one by one. Sara walked closer and slipped each flower into a separate vase, the florist in her not wanting to see innocent flowers go to waste as the man from the dining room, Ian's mother, and Kat's mother walked into the living room to see what was happening. Ian reached deep into the royal blue vase and smirked. "Who sends flowers without watering them?"

"I was thinking the same thing," Sara said, as she slipped the last carnation into a vase. "None of these flowers are damp."

"That's because water would tamper with this." Ian slid his hand out and held a small bugging device. He held it in the palm of his hand. "It's not activated though."

"How can you tell?" Kat asked.

"Because this type of bug has a small red light that flicks on. Low budget." Ian pointed to a small spot. As soon as he did, the bug lit up with a small red reflector light. He moved his finger to his lips to motion to everyone not to say anything.

"Wow, Kat, nice flowers. Who are they from?" he asked, as if the conversation was just happening. Kat smirked and sat up straight. "I don't know. It seems I have a secret admirer. Jealous?" She asked playfully making him grin and lightly squeeze her knee before continuing.

"I bet they are from Marshall," Travis stated. "He just can't take a hint."

"Ugh, I hope not." The disgust from Kat was genuine and therefore made their scene sound like reality. She grabbed a notepad and wrote quickly, "Can I destroy the bug?"

Ian looked to Travis and they both nodded.

"I think I will add a bit more water to the vase though. The petals are looking droopy," Kat stated as Ian dropped the bug in a glass of water Travis provided. They watched as the small red light slowly faded. Once it was out, Travis took the bug out and stomped on it. "Well done, Kat. Makes them think we didn't discover it, but also hinders them from hearing our conversations." Travis ruffled her hair.

"Which one of them would be bugging me?"

"Biggs." Ian and Travis said at the same time.

"But why?"

"To see if we discuss the necklace," Travis supplied. "It makes sense. He wants to know our plans or if we are even on to him and the jewels."

Kat rubbed her face and felt her mom sit down beside her and pull her into a firm squeeze.

"I'm getting tired of this," she admitted.

"We know, Sweetie." Her mom rubbed her arm. "But it is almost over. The award's ceremony is Friday. You will go. You will wear that gorgeous dress. You will wear the necklace. And you will bring down the biggest drug lord on the east coast."

"Wow Mom, you sure do know how to give a pep talk," Kat muttered before her mom laughed. "I've spent too many years as a police chief's wife. Your daddy would say to buck up, pull up your boot straps and do what needs to be done."

"You're right, he would." Kat took a deep breath and looked to Ian and Travis. "Alright boys, fill me in on your plan." Her gaze darted to the other man, who up until now had remained in the dining room. "Oh, and by the way," Kat added, motioning towards him, "who is this guy?"

Everyone laughed as he stepped forward. "Dr. Richard O'Dell, my apologies for not introducing myself sooner."

Her brows lifted and her eyes set on Ian. "Your dad?"

He nodded. "My mom was a little worried about me earlier and she called in reinforcements. We aren't so different in that regard." He motioned towards his mother.

Kat shook his dad's hand. "It is nice to meet you, Mr. O'Dell. You have a pretty remarkable son."

Kat's compliment took Ian by surprise as well as his parents. Her honesty shocked them all.

"Well, thank you, Kat."

She stood and walked towards the kitchen. "Your spaghetti is about to burn, Sara."

"Shoot!" Sara ran after her towards the kitchen, her friend's lack of prowess in the kitchen making the group smile. "Saved it!" Sara called as the sounds of a dish setting upon the counter sounded through the room. "Everything is almost ready. Kat, the table." She pointed for Kat to set the table and Kat immediately set about the task. When she was finished, she slipped from the room to her bedroom to call and check in with Jeremiah and Anna.

"Hey you," she greeted. "Fill me in."

"He's doing great. Doctors think he will only need to stay a couple more days, and that is just to keep an eye on him. Otherwise, your dad is as healthy as a horse. The bullet tore through some muscle, but nothing overly serious," Jeremiah reported. "How are you holding up?"

"I'm doing fine, and that's good to hear. Thanks for being there, Jer. I can't tell you how thankful I am."

"Kat, you don't even have to mention it. I would do anything for you, you know that."

"I know." A smile laced her voice as she slowly pulled on a small thread on the bed comforter.

"You're awfully quiet. Is that all you needed? Or do you need to talk?"

"Yes, and yes, although I'm not sure where to start or what I want to talk about." She heard him snicker through the phone.

"O'Dell." Jeremiah stated. "It's okay if you need to talk about him, Kat. I won't think less of you if you have fallen for the man. Super man had Lois Lane. Iron man had Pepper Potts. Batman had Catwoman."

Laughing, Kat sniffled as she fought back tears of relief at a regular conversation that required nothing but fun. "All true. Are you saying Ian is a superhero?"

"To you he is, and if he keeps you safe through all this, he is to me as well."

"I can't imagine him in tights." Kat jested as Jeremiah continued on about his obsession with comic book heroes. Kat noticed a movement by the door and looked up to find Ian standing there. She cleared her throat. "Listen, I need to go. I still need to call Anna and check in." She paused and listened before smiling. "Thanks again, Jeremiah. Love you. Bye." She hung up and grinned. "Is the food ready?"

Ian nodded and walked into the room. "You okay?" He swiped his thumb over her cheek where a tear still lingered.

"Oh," Kat swiped her cheeks and smiled, "yes, I'm fine. Jeremiah was just updating me on my dad."

"Everything well?"

"Yes. Thankfully." She stood and began walking towards the door. "We should eat. I never got lunch, and I have no idea if you and Travis did either. I'm starving." Without a backwards glance, she left the room.

∞

Dinner had been relaxing despite the tense circumstances that had brought everyone around the same table. Ian's parents made Kat smile as they shared stories about Ian when he was younger, and her mother matched their stories with equal embarrassment for Kat. Travis and Sara shared their own stories, and before anyone knew it, the night had progressed, the hour was late, and the lighted candles nearly smoldered out within the puddled wax. Kat stood to refill her glass of water and instinctively counted the other half empty or empty glasses at the table. She was in and out of the kitchen in silent movement and had all glasses refilled before anyone realized she had left the table.

"You just can't shut it off, can you?" Ian whispered, as their parents continued to converse.

A chagrined smile washed over her face. "Habit."

He winked at her before turning his attention back to his mother.

"I wish I could be here the night of the awards ceremony. It's been years since I've seen Ian wear a tuxedo. And Kat, that dress," she placed her hand over her heart and feigned a fainting spell. "You two will look so lovely."

"We could always show up and take pictures," Kat's mom interrupted.

"Like prom." Mrs. O'Dell nodded enthusiastically and then laughed as she noted the horrified looks on Kat and Ian's faces. "Kidding. Only kidding, loves." She cast a sly glance towards Kat's mother before returning to the conversation. "Though I must say it is a shame the beautiful dress and nice suit are having to be used under false pretenses."

"What do you mean, Mom?" Ian asked. "They are for the awards ceremony." He shook his head as if she did not understand and waited until Kat stood before turning towards Travis and his father.

"Need some help?" Sara asked, as Kat began to sneak her way towards the kitchen to clean up.

Kat shook her head. "No thanks. You visit."

Recognizing her friend's need for alone time, Sara smiled in reassurance as she continued conversing with the moms. If Kat and Ian were not careful, their mothers would have their entire life together planned out. Though the thought made Sara want to squeal with glee, she also knew Kat did not like to feel cornered or pushed into a decision. The way Kat and Ian's relationship had progressed towards a friendship had been organic and smooth. She hated to see that disappear with too much meddling. She watched as Ian excused himself from the table and made his way towards the kitchen as well. Though he exited quietly, his presence and destination did not go unnoticed by the older women, who held such high hopes for their children's developing relationship.

Ian watched as Kat slid the glass dish under the hot water, the steam rising up and slightly curling the tendrils of hair at her temples. She was beautiful, and for the first time tonight, he saw a relaxation settle over her shoulders. *She was at home in the kitchen,* he thought. The peace she had in her café during their all-night prep session carried over to the present and he saw the sheer joy in her service as she set the clean dish aside and started washing another. He leaned against the cabinet behind her, his arms crossed, his presence unnoticed as she continued. When the last dish was washed, she reached for a hand towel and began to dry them. The monotonous task of cleaning dishes had never appealed to him more. She sighed as she dried the last dish and began opening cabinets, her task almost finished. When she turned, she jumped in surprise at his presence and almost dropped the dish she held. She fumbled it in her hands and regained her composure. "You scared me." Breathless, she placed one of her hands over her heart before continuing her way to the appropriate cabinet. She opened the cabinet next to his head and slid the glass dish inside, stacking it within like dishes. When she closed the cabinet door, she looked to him. "Was there something you needed?" she asked.

He reached for her hand, smoothing his thumb over her wrist. "No. I just needed to take a breather from all the conversation in the dining room."

"You mean you wanted our meddling mothers to stop harassing you?" Her lips tilted into a knowing smile as she withdrew her hand from his and crossed her arms. "What do we do now?" she asked.

Unsure if she meant about them or about the case, he asked, "About?"

"About the awards ceremony. I mean, my dad is in the hospital and I know you guys were hoping he could help with surveillance."

Slight disappointment settled in his chest, but Ian knew her focus on the case was what should have been his focus as well. Shaking away his wishful thoughts, he resettled against the cabinets. "We have plenty of coverage to keep you safe. However, I do want to give you the choice to back out, Kat. You do not have to attend if you do not want to."

"Oh, I want to." She confirmed. "I wouldn't miss it. Plus, I cannot wait to see the look on Marshall's face when he sees the necklace."

"And I will be right beside you all night. I won't let you out of my sight, so if at any point you become scared or nervous, just let me know."

She unfolded her arms and slipped them around his waist and gave him a small squeeze. "I know. Thanks, Ian."

He slowly returned her hug and nodded before she slipped away and continued putting away dishes. "Well, I guess I will try to round up my parents and subtly hint that it is time for them to leave."

Kat grinned. "They're really great, Ian. You're lucky."

"Yeah, they are pretty special. A bit invasive at times," he grinned as she softly laughed.

"What parents aren't?" she asked with a shrug of her shoulders.

"Fair point." He held her gaze a moment longer and then reached out to cup her cheek in his hand. Saying nothing, he let his hand fall gently from her face, then turned towards the dining room, his mother's welcome full of tenderness as he draped his arm over the back of her chair as he sat.

∞

The next two days were full of planning. Acting out different scenarios and possible threats had left Kat exhausted, but the foolproof plan for the night of the ceremony left her feeling encouraged that all the danger would soon be coming to an end. She glanced up as Sara stepped

Katharine E. Hamilton

out of the bathroom, her hair and make up polished and ready for the big night. "Well?" Sara asked, turning slowly so Kat could see the back of her hair. "What do you think?"

"Love it," Kat complimented. "How'd you do that?" She asked, lightly touching the intricate twist at the back of Sara's head.

"With patience. My arms are killing me from holding them up for so long." Laughing, Sara walked towards the closet and slipped her dress out of its plastic protection. "You going to start getting ready? We only have an hour before the limo arrives."

Kat reluctantly made her way into the bathroom and began unraveling the sloppy bun off the top of her head. She then began work curling and fastening her hair into a half up and half down mound of rich mahogany. Her cascading curls would flood down her exposed back and fill the void of bare skin her dress displayed. *Glamorous*, that's how she felt and as she whisked the last flick of her mascara over her smoky eye shadowed gaze. She felt the nerves begin to rise up as she slipped into her dress. The silk fabric draped over her skin and she slipped into her heels. A knock sounded on the bedroom door before Sara entered. Her friend froze, blue eyes wide and mouth ajar. "Kat," Sara's voice a whisper, "you look stunning."

Kat nervously ran a hand over her hair. "You think so?"

"I am absolutely speechless. Gorgeous." Sara stepped forward and squeezed her hands. "Where's the necklace?"

"Ian has it. I'm assuming he will give it to me in the car."

"Speaking of, the car is here. Travis wanted me to come and get you. Ian is doing the sweep now and making sure our exit is safe. He will meet us at the limo." Sara linked her hand with Kat's. "Ready?"

"As I'll ever be." Kat whispered a silent prayer for strength as she and Sara made their way down the hallway. Travis stood, handsome and tall in his black tuxedo waiting in the living room. His gaze travelled over Sara once more before looking at Kat. A slow smile spread over his face. "You ladies are going to kill every man in sight tonight. You both are drop dead gorgeous." He lightly kissed Kat's cheek before walking them both towards the front door. "O'Dell gave the all clear." Travis opened the door and stepped out, followed by Sara. Kat hovered a moment, mustering up her last ounce of courage as she took a deep breath and stepped out into the evening. The long black vehicle parked along the curb awaited her, but the man standing next to it was the only thing that stood out to her. Ian turned as she stepped out onto the front porch and froze. She watched as the

Katharine E. Hamilton

driver attempted to continue their conversation, but upon noticing Ian's attention being diverted, trailed off with a knowing smile as he slipped behind the wheel.

∞

Ian lightly tugged at the collar of his shirt, as he spotted Kat. She was a vision, and his heart raced and should anyone listen closely, he knew they would hear it pounding in his chest. She was beautiful, beyond beautiful, and he inwardly wished their evening together could be more than a case. He noticed her eyes searching his, uncertainty in their depths as she stepped in front of him. They stood for a moment, neither speaking as they surveyed one another. His hand betrayed him and he lightly brushed his knuckles over her smooth cheek. "Ready?" he asked.

She nodded, but not before the light spark in her eyes dimmed and a flash of disappointment washed over her face. He knew he should have complimented her, but what was he to say? That she stole his breath away? That she was the most beautiful woman he had ever seen? He physically struggled to maintain his even breathing as she brushed passed him to slide into the limo. Her perfume lingered behind her, the light vanilla scent of her fragrance tormenting him. He caught Travis' amused smile and shook his head. Travis slapped him on the shoulder. "Not bad, huh?"

With a grunt, Ian slid into the car. Kat sat in the middle of the farthest seat and he slid next to her. Reaching into his pocket, he pulled out the necklace box. "I think it's time we put this on you," he said, as he opened the box and retrieved the delicate diamonds. "Allow me."

She turned slightly and he draped the necklace around her slender neck, his fingers lightly brushing her skin as he clasped it beneath her hair. When she turned, the diamonds caught speckles of light and sparkled around her neck. The beauty of the diamonds paled in comparison to Kat herself, but he kept his words to himself as the car pulled away from the curb.

"Everyone remember the plan for this evening?" Travis asked.

Kat nodded. Though she was not excited about continuing her act as Ian's girlfriend, she was excited to see if her café brought the award home for the 'Hottest Spot in the City.'

"You look beautiful, Sara," She complimented again as she watched her friend fuss over her hair and fidget in her seat. Sara blushed.

"Doesn't she?" Travis leaned over and kissed Sara's lips in a light, but intimate kiss that had Kat thinking wistful thoughts. One day, she supposed, she would find such a relationship where quiet moments could be found, even in the midst of chaos and company. Ian's phone rang and he immediately answered. His brisk tone settled a morose mood over the vehicle as he echoed orders and commands from the chief upon their arrival. Kat could recite the overall plan in her sleep, they had rehearsed it so many times. But one thing bothered her as she felt the weight of the necklace around her neck like shackles. Why all of this for a necklace? No matter how beautiful or expensive, she could not shake the feeling that the piece of jewelry was not the reason she was under attack. Thinking back to her relationship with Marshall, she tried to conjure up any memory that might explain why she was a target, but she continued to come up empty. Nothing stood out to her. She would often visit him at work, but there was nothing out of the ordinary that she remembered. It was a typical office. Dark, quiet, and other than a friendly secretary, Kat's interaction with his coworkers was slim. She tried to think of social functions she and Marshall attended, and again, nothing stood out. She flinched when Ian squeezed her hand. "We're here. Ready?" he asked.

She nodded, still not sure her courage had followed along for the ride to the ceremony. Ian tilted her chin up to look her in the eye. She noted the concern in his and tried to muster a smile.

Sara and Travis slinked out of the vehicle and Kat waited for Ian to move so they could

Katharine E. Hamilton

follow. He continued to sit and stare at her. "Should we go in?" she asked quietly.

He leaned forward and brushed his lips over hers. Soft, tender, and quick. Surprise lit her face and he mustered a small groan as he slid a hand through his hair, the golden mane tamed as best as could be managed, but the unruliness remained, and she found it charming. "May I escort you, Ms. Riesling?" he asked, as he slid out of the vehicle and offered his hand to help her exit. When she stepped from the vehicle, camera flashes surrounded them and she offered a genuine smile of surprise as several reporters asked her questions about her dress and her necklace. Ian linked her arm with his as they slowly made their way to the entrance of the grand hotel. When they cleared the doorway and entered the lavish ballroom, Kat let her eyes settle upon the exquisite table settings and the chandeliers that hung over ornate wall dressings and beautiful draperies. The entire room breathed elegance and sophistication and she felt out of her element. Though she had been to the festivities before, the overwhelming sense of luxury and opulence seemed foreign to her. "You alright?"

Ian's words brushed against her hair as he leaned over to speak to her. She glanced up at him and nodded. "Yes. Why?"

He pointed at her hand linked in his arm and noticed how tightly she was gripping his arm. She forced her hand to relax. "A bit nervous, I guess," she admitted quietly. A soft smile flashed over his handsome face and he leaned down towards her, turning her to face him. He brought his hands to her shoulders and lightly held her in place. "You are going to do fine, and I am going to keep you safe. You look," he paused as his gaze wandered over her, "breathtaking." He looked away for a moment and then back down at her. "Truly."

She reached up and grabbed his hands from her shoulders and kept one hand clasped in his as she turned towards their table. "We should sit. Marshall and his group have arrived." Her voice was void of emotion as she walked towards their table, a handful of people stopping them along the way to congratulate her on her nomination and to compliment her dress. She was pleased with Ian's reaction. Though he had not said much, she saw the look in his eyes when he gazed at her. It probably mirrored her own, she realized, when she looked at him. He made quite a picture all cleaned up, and she realized in that instant, she wanted him to dress up more often. He pulled out her chair and she sat, Sara and Travis opposite her, and Ian sat beside her. "I hope you win tonight," he whispered in her ear and caused chills to race up her arms. He noticed and a small smile tugged at his lips as he reached for her hand.

Katharine E. Hamilton

A speaker, lanky in stride and dressed in a white suit, walked to center stage and applause sounded throughout the banquet hall. He waved and smiled, tossed out his opening lines and jokes, and then centered in on the reason everyone was gathered. "Ladies and Gentlemen!" The speaker began. "We are so honored you all could make it tonight to the 47th Chicago's Best Awards. We are grateful to the Draden Hotel for hosting again this year. We will begin serving drinks now. Please enjoy yourselves, and let us see who ranks amongst Chicago's Best!" Everyone clapped. "Please welcome to the stage, Mayor Leadlow!"

Kat felt her stomach tighten in nerves, but she clapped along with everyone else. The mayor began speaking about the history of the awards. Kat tuned out as she let her eyes roam the room. She saw Marshall's table. He was watching the mayor intently. She observed the men and women sitting at his table and was surprised by some of the people.

Ian could see Kat searching the room and her forehead furrowed. "You okay?" He leaned and whispered in her ear. She jolted in surprise and then smiled. She let out a deep breath and turned towards him. Their faces were inches apart. "I'm fine, thanks."

Ian leaned forward and lightly brushed his lips on her forehead. Kat's eyes closed with the intimacy of his actions. She felt her pulse speed up. When she opened her eyes, they were met with Ian's sharp, green gaze. Ian pulled back in his chair and relaxed. Kat turned her attention back to the stage, even though her mind wandered to wishful thoughts of Ian and herself after this investigation was over.

∞

Ian noticed the second Marshall spotted Kat wearing the necklace, for the man did a quick double take before staring for a full five minutes in disbelief. Ian caught his eye and nodded politely, though he truly wished he could knock his teeth in. Kat squeezed his hand and she offered a nervous smile as a man and woman took the stage.

The time had come for the final award to be announced, and Kat gripped Sara's hand on one side, and Ian's on the other. Should either woman win the award, Ian knew everyone at the table would be pleased. "We are so excited to be handing out this last award. An award that is the Holy Grail of awards tonight. "The Hottest Spot in the City" represents the business that the residents of Chicago feel is the best place to go. This particular place jumped on the radar several years ago. When you walk in to this business, you are greeted by cheerful smiles and great customer service. Along with its treats and delicious delicacies, when you leave you know you are going to have a better day. Ladies and Gentlemen, for the third year in a row... "The Hottest Spot in the City" award goes to Kat Riesling and Kat's Corner Café!"

The entire place erupted into applause. Kat stood and Sara embraced her.

Ian hugged her tightly and cupped her chin. They stared into each other's eyes a moment before a large grin spread over her face and she pulled away to accept Travis' hug and to wind her way towards the stage. Ian caught Travis' eye, both men surveying the crowds to make sure no one seemed out of the ordinary as Kat hugged the woman presenter and shook the hand of the man. She stepped to the microphone.

"Thank you so much!" she exclaimed with a thousand-watt smile.

"I honestly do not know what to say. I am so grateful. I cannot tell you how much this means to me. I want to thank Jeremiah, who sadly could not be here tonight, but who has been my number one employee from the beginning. He's my biggest supporter and hardest worker, and I would not be standing here today without his help." People applauded. "I also want to thank my friends that are here with me tonight. I am so fortunate to have such loving people in my life. And of course, our customers for voting. We love you all, and have so much fun with you. Thank you for coming to see us each morning and brightening *our* day." The audience applauded as she was escorted off of the stage to the backstage area.

∞

"We have security coverage for backstage," Travis reminded him as Ian was about to stand. "She will be fine."

"That was the last award." Ian whispered. "What now?"

"There's the banquet in the ballroom next door for about an hour or so, then we head to the café. But we have to make sure the banquet is where we see Thompson's reaction towards Kat. If anything is going to happen, it will happen there." Travis stood as Kat reached the table with a happy smile and shaky hands as she handed her award to him to look at. Sara grabbed her in a tight hug and squeal as Kat slinked towards her seat next to Ian. Ian grabbed her around the waist before she could sit and smiled down at her. "Congratulations, Kat."

Breathless at his sudden move, Kat's thanks was muted behind the sound of a long exhale as he lightly kissed her cheek.

He heard the speakers over the intercom, but didn't hear what was being said. Kat had stolen his world...and his heart.

Her eyes met his and she could tell something had changed between them in that moment. She gave a shy smile and then slowly slid into her chair.

«CHAPTER TWELVE»

THE NEXT BALLROOM OVER consisted of a live band, dance floor, more drinks, and mingling. Kat did not have to work her way around the room too much because everyone came to her and congratulated her. Ian stood close by her side and was greeted by everyone that came to give their good graces. Kat saw Marshall making his way towards her. She talked with Sara as she heard him approach.

"Look alive everyone." Travis muttered.

Kat turned. "Marshall. Hello," she stated with a false smile. Ian had walked off to get drinks in order to give Marshall an opportunity to approach Kat.

"Congratulations, Kat. Three years in a row is quite a feat. Here, I think it's worthy of a toast." He stated, and handed Kat a glass of champagne. She took it politely. He slightly raised his glass and took a sip. She took a sip of hers as well.

"Thank you, Marshall," she replied.

"Tell me," he began, and draped his arm around her waist turning their backs to the others. "What made you decide to finally wear your necklace? And that dress... well, I have to say, this is the first time I've seen you look so stunning."

Kat forced a polite smile. "Well, it's amazing what a woman can come up with, when she wants to."

Marshall took the insult with a forced smile and an angry laugh. "Yes, well, I guess I just never thought I would see that necklace again."

Ian walked up and held two glasses of champagne.

"Oh, hello again," he interrupted, towering over Marshall. Ian grabbed the glass out of Kat's hands and replaced it with a new one. She graciously accepted and linked her arm thru his.

"Hey Sweetie," she said. "You remember Marshall Thompson?"

Ian acted as if nothing seemed out of the ordinary and stuck out his hand. "Of course, good to see you."

Marshall shook his hand firmly with a forced smile. "Yes, of course."

Kat could tell Marshall's patience was wearing thin and that he did not appreciate Ian barging into their conversation. "I must go, but it was nice to see you Kat." Marshall nodded towards Ian and slowly migrated his way across the ballroom.

"Well?" Ian whispered. "Anything?"

"He asked about the necklace," Kat commented, "but he didn't seem bothered by my wearing it."

"I'm not so sure. I caught him staring at it throughout the ceremony."

"Perhaps in disbelief that I would actually wear it," Kat added. "I honestly don't feel it's what he's after."

"Hey," Ian thumbed her chin. "Let me worry about that. I hear you are to be dancing the night away." Winking, he set his glass down and offered his hand. Kat obliged with a smile, and he drew her out to the dance floor, her dress whispering at her heels.

He twirled her before pulling her to him. She rested her hand behind his neck as he slipped his hand around her back. A slow dance was the perfect time to play up their relationship. Kat fell into step with Ian and they moved gracefully across the dance floor. Ian's hand rested on her bare back and he couldn't help but relish the touch of her soft skin. He could feel her pulse quicken in the hand he still held. She lightly began to play with his hair that brushed the collar of his shirt behind his neck. Ian leaned his forehead against hers as he let go of her hand and brought his down to her side as well. She wrapped her other arm around his neck as well and stepped closer towards him. Soon her body was lightly pressed against his and her head rested upon his chest as they danced.

"Kat," he whispered. She gave a small sound to let him know she was listening.

"I want you to know that you really do look gorgeous tonight." He said quietly.

She smiled to herself. "Thanks," she whispered back.

"I also want you to know that..." he paused, realizing that the time and place should be different before he continued his next statement.

Katharine E. Hamilton

"Yes?" she softly asked.

"Nevermind," he commented quiet.

The song ended, but Kat did not seem to notice. She continued to lightly sway and keep her body pressed against Ian. He did not want to end the moment. She felt so right in his arms. His pulse began to quicken. He then slightly shifted and she raised her head and smiled. She gave a small bow. He lightly linked his fingers with hers and walked her back towards their friends.

"Ready for the after party?" Sara asked with a wide smile. "I'm ready to blow this joint and eat some real food."

Kat placed her hand on her heart, "Why Sara, that is the best compliment a girl could hear. I'll text and give Jeremiah a heads-up that we are headed that way and that he can go ahead and start serving drinks to the other guests."

Ian leaned over to hear the plan and Kat turned her head slightly to smile at him and their eyes met. Feeling the effects of the night, Kat could not help but smile at him. She lightly gave him a peck on the lips. Surprised, Ian pulled his head back in shock but then gave a small smile. Kat winked at him and then turned back to a beaming Sara.

∞

The drive to the café was quick and uneventful, and Ian was not sure what to make of their temporary safety. The awards night was the best chance to get to Kat and yet, no one had made a move. Thompson, though rude, seemed too aloof throughout the night, and his focus was not on Kat for most of the evening. *What did they miscalculate?* Ian wondered. *What had he missed?* Ian and Kat pulled into the parking lot of the cafe and Ian stepped out of the vehicle first. He looked around, noticed a few other officers hidden here and there, but no sign of Marshall Thompson or Biggs' men. He then reached his hand into the car to help Kat emerge. She clasped his hand and stepped out of the car. Ian escorted her to the door of the shop. Kat briefly stopped him from entering. She turned her eyes to his and gave him a small, nervous smile. Ian returned it. "You okay?" he asked.

Kat nodded. "Yes, sorry, just wanted to take a quick breath," she whispered. "For some reason, I'm more nervous now than I was at the ceremony."

Ian smiled. "Kat, you have nothing to be nervous about. These people are here because they love you and want to celebrate with you. Simple as that."

Kat gave him a grateful smile and then nodded for him to open the door.

∞

As soon as she stepped inside, corks popped all at once and everyone cheered and clapped for her. She lifted her award in the air and walked it over to the shelf behind the register counter, and placed it next to the previous two. Everyone cheered. Kat beamed and took the glass of champagne Jeremiah offered her. Soon, music was playing and hors d'oeuvres were being passed, and the party had started. Kat perched on a stool and began talking with Sara while people danced and mingled. Her mother walked up and embraced her. "Oh Sweetie, I am so proud of you." She squeezed Kat's hands and motioned towards Kat's father sitting in a booth. His complexion was paler than normal, but he looked healthy. He was recovering well, and the tension in her heart eased a bit. She noticed Ian speaking with him, the two men oblivious to the party surrounding them as whatever their topic of discussion was dominated their attention. "He's a good man," her mother whispered. "And he cares for you."

"Mom," Kat warned in a soft whisper as her gaze then saw Ian's parents walking towards her. Surprise lit her eyes as Ian's mother enveloped her in a hug. "You look beautiful, Kat, so beautiful. I knew that dress was worth saving." Mrs. O'Dell scrunched up her shoulders with a small smile before gently rubbing her husband's back. He offered his hand. "Good to see you, dear. Congratulations on your achievement." Formality, something she had noticed when he mingled in her house, was Mr. O'Dell's signature trait, and she smiled at its pleasantness. "Thank you, Mr. O'Dell. I am so glad you two were able to join us tonight."

"Of course, dear," Mrs. O'Dell continued. "I was not about to miss my boy being all dressed up."

Sharing a laugh, Kat's mother walked away with the O'Dells and Sara eased next to her.

"So..." Sara began. "I have this feeling that you and Ian had some sparks flying between you all night. Am I right?" she asked as she sipped from her champagne flute, trying to hide her smile.

Kat sighed, and a worried expression flashed across her face.

"What's wrong?" Sara asked, concern flooding her voice. She stared at her friend with worry.

Kat gave a small smile towards her friend. "Nothing is wrong," she answered softly, as her gaze moved across the room to where Ian stood laughing with Travis.

"It was a great night, despite the whole hidden agenda to catch Marshall in the act of something. I wondered if Ian and Travis noticed anything out of the ordinary, but neither has said anything to me. You think they would?"

"Yes. Honestly, I think they were surprised nothing happened. Travis said Ian was concerned about the ride back here, but nothing happened. Seems he has relaxed a bit." Sara nodded towards Ian as he meandered around the room talking with different people. "Everything with Ian tonight felt so real. It was so easy to lean on him, depend on him, kiss him even. I had to keep reminding myself he and I are just acting. That this charade is almost over." Sara gave her friend's hand a squeeze. "Don't be so sure about that."

Kat rolled her eyes in disbelief.

"Believe me," Sara continued. "Have you seen the way he looks at you?" Sara asked with conviction.

Sara continued to look at her friend. "Kat, he is so in love with you, it's obvious to everyone but you.

Kat gave a small laugh. "Love? I don't think so. Remember, once this case is finished our relationship is as well."

Sara reached for two new glasses of champagne and handed one to Kat. "Let's stop pity partying and get the real party started. Now drink up Kat. It's your night to shine." She wiggled her eyebrows as they both giggled and tapped their glasses in a toast.

∞

At one o'clock in the morning, Kat looked to Jeremiah as a signal that she was ready to wrap the party up. Jeremiah spoke into a microphone and pulled the attention to himself. "Ladies and gentlemen, we thank you so much for coming out tonight to honor our favorite gal, Kat Riesling!" Everyone cheered and clapped. Jeremiah raised his glass to her in a salute. "However, it is getting late and we have to open in four hours." People laughed and nodded. "So thank you all for coming, but we are calling it a successful night. Please be careful going home, and if you need a place for breakfast in the morning, think about us." He smiled and gave one last toast as people began saying their goodbyes. Kat stood at the door as people walked out, shaking hands and hugging several as they left her with good wishes. She had lost count of how much champagne she had consumed throughout the night. Her entire body felt relaxed and heavy. She definitely could fall into a deep sleep at the moment. Travis came up to her as the last guests left. He gave her a friendly hug. Ian walked up. "Okay Kat, it is time to get you to the car and escort you home."

Kat stood a little straighter and held her hand to her forehead like a salute, but held it in place as if imitating a military soldier at full alert. Sara laughed beside her. Kat began mocking Ian's tone of voice. "Time to get you to the car and escort you home." She giggled half way thru the last few words causing Sara and herself to stumble over each other as they laughed.

"Seriously ladies, we need to get you guys home." Travis stated.

Kat stood a little straighter. "Let me go check the back really quickly to make sure the switches to the stove are off, and then we can leave," she stated.

"Jeremiah will see to that," Travis stated firmly.

Kat's giggling halted at his answer. Travis knew she took her shop seriously, and to leave without checking on things was not her style, even if she was tired. She lightly tapped his face with her hand, which actually ended up being more forceful than necessary.

"Go check on things Kat, and then we leave," Ian stated decisively.

She nodded and walked thru the kitchen's swinging door. The remaining attendees gave Ian a smile and exchanged their farewells as they headed home. "We'll head on home. See you in a few?" Travis asked.

"Right behind you," Ian replied as he glanced at his watch. Kat should be back by now. He walked over and opened the kitchen doors to see two men, one with his arms wrapped around Kat, one hand over her mouth as she bucked and jumped to try and release herself. The other man held the door to the freezer open and Ian yelled. "Hey! Freeze where you are!"

The two men smirked and threw Kat into the freezer slamming the door before Ian could utter another word. Ian charged at them. He dodged a blow to the stomach and took down the first man with one swing connecting to his nose. The other man swung a few punches, one landing in Ian's side. He flinched briefly, but continued to fight. He reached his arm back and suddenly was hit in the back of the head with something. He fell to the ground as his vision blurred. He felt his body being hoisted into the freezer and tossed on the floor. He saw Kat's concerned gaze before he lost consciousness.

∞

Kat did not even see the men coming. How could she miss the signs that something wasn't right? And now Ian was thrown inside the freezer as well. She stared at him as he groaned and collapsed. Panicked, she rolled him over and gently placed his head on the floor. She jumped to her feet and ran to the small glass window in the door. Marshall Thompson stuck his ugly face in the opening. He had a snarl and smile on his face. "I'm terribly sorry Kat, but it seems that you've gotten yourself in a bit of a pickle," he laughed.

Kat beat on the door furiously.

"No need Kat. No one is here but me. They have all left you in the hands of your obviously gifted detective there. That one... on the floor." He laughed again. Kat turned a concerned gaze to Ian. She could hear Marshall laughing.

"You see, Kat, all of this could have been avoided if you had just given me the jump drive."

"I have no idea what you're talking about!" she screamed as she pounded on the glass. His eyes changed for a moment and then hardened in disbelief.

"Do not play dumb with me!" he yelled. "You snatched it from my office." Marshall raised his hand as if holding someone back, and Kat noticed two men holding red gasoline containers.

"That jump drive was my insurance. My upper hand!" Marshall continued. "And thanks to you, Biggs no longer trusts me. Until I receive the jump drive, he will not allow me to represent him or his men. Do you know how much money I was being paid?! Of course you do," he continued, "you have the jump drive and all of that is on there.

"Losing Biggs' trust will be the end of me. Now tell me where the jump drive is, Kat." His eyes were fierce, and she shot a nervous glance towards Ian as Marshall turned the temperature gauge down. "Best hurry, Kat. I would hate for you to freeze." His smirk was diabolical, and her stomach knotted.

"I do not have a jump drive, Marshall," she called through the door. "I have no idea what you are talking about. I thought you wanted the necklace back." She ripped the diamonds off of her neck and held it up. She noted the concern that flashed over his face. He believed her, and yet, he did not know what to make of her holding the diamonds as if they meant nothing.

"I don't believe you," he hissed. "Burn it down." Kat watched as the men began dousing her kitchen in gasoline. "Thanks to you, Kat, my world has crumbled. The only fair thing for me to do is to let you watch your life crumble as well." He made direct eye contact with Kat thru the glass and smiled a smile that chilled her more than the freezer temperatures. He saw her shudder.

"Have fun watching your café burn... from inside the freezer." He adjusted the temperature knob to well below freezing. "You will see your cafe burn to ashes. If the fire does get hot enough to burn you in there... well, so be it. I'm going to give you thirty minutes in there, so you can get good and frosty, then I will let the fire take you over. Give my regards to Detective O'Dell there." Marshall gave her one last evil smile, and then he disappeared. Kat gazed thru the glass as she saw her beautiful kitchen getting drenched in gasoline.

Ian groaned and she frantically turned and knelt beside him. It was definitely getting colder in the freezer. She was kicking herself for wearing a piece of silk and calling it a dress. She was going to get cold and fast. She helped Ian sit up.

"Kat, are you okay?" Ian asked as he held his head in his hand.

Kat gave a small smile but her worried eyes betrayed her. "We're locked in the freezer. Marshall lowered the temperature and he's burning down my cafe."

Ian's eyes widened and he bolted to his feet. He paced a few steps and pulled out his cell phone. Naturally, he did not have any service standing in a metal freezer. He paced some more as he tried to figure out his next move. He glanced out the window and saw Marshall Thompson standing near the back door of the cafe and his men carrying gasoline cartons outside.

"He said he's giving me thirty minutes before he sets it on fire. I guess he wants me to freeze to death before lighting the match to thaw me back out," Kat commented dryly. Her teeth began to chatter. Her entire body shook and she could feel her ribs beginning to ache.

Ian, finally breaking his silence, looked over at her and then realized her condition. He mentally kicked himself. She definitely must be freezing in her thin dress. He walked over to her and stripped off his jacket. Kat held up her hands. "What are you doing?" she asked in surprise.

"You're freezing, Kat. You need heat. I have long sleeves on... Come here." He pulled her to him and wrapped his jacket around her shoulders. Kat could already feel the heat from his jacket seeping into her body.

"He wasn't after the necklace," she explained, her teeth clicking together as she spoke.

"What?" Ian asked.

"He thinks I stole a jump drive from his office that has pertinent information on it. Information showing how much Biggs has paid him for representing some of his cases." She watched as the information sank in and Ian's gaze intensified.

"I have no idea what he is even referring to, Ian. I never took anything from his office. How could I? I was never alone in there. I was always talking with his secretary before he would take me into his office. I would never have had the opportunity, even if I did know of its existence."

Ian slowly lowered his arms. Her body continued to shake but not as bad. "So he is tying up loose ends just in case you're lying. Killing you kills any information you may know about it."

"But I don't know anything!" Her voice pleaded in panic and he squeezed her shaking hands. "I believe you, Kat, but he doesn't, and right now our only focus needs to be on an escape. Think Kat. Is there any way out of here?" he asked.

Kat shook her head. "No... I mean, the reason I got this freezer in the first place was because the last one broke and locked me in and Jeremiah is terrible about locking himself inside the freezer. He even went as far as buying us one of those tracker phones... WAIT!" She ran to the back of the freezer and began rustling around. She came back with what looked like a military walkie-talkie.

"What is that?" Ian asked.

"It's some sort of gadget Jeremiah found. It's like a GPS or tracker phone that hikers use. It's able to withstand severe temperatures. He didn't want to have to worry about one of us getting locked in the freezer again, so he put one in here. We have two phone numbers programmed in it. Mine and his." She switched it on and it came to life. She gave a big smile to Ian. She dialed Jeremiah's phone number and handed the phone to Ian.

Jeremiah's voice rang out.

"Hello? Kat? Everything okay?" he asked.

"Jeremiah, it's Ian. Listen to me and do exactly what I tell you to do. Marshall Thompson and his men are here. They have locked Kat and me in the freezer and they are going to torch the place in about... 23 minutes," he added, looking at his watch. "I need you to first, call the fire department. Then I want you to call Travis and the chief and let them know the situation. Under *no* circumstances are you to come here yourself. Do you understand?" Ian finished.

"Already on it. Had you on speaker phone, so Travis is on the phone with the chief, and Sara has just placed the call to the fire department. Are you guys okay? Kat?" he asked, worry in his voice.

"I'm fine, Jeremiah," she called out.

"We're okay for now, but Thompson has lowered the temperature to below freezing, so time is of the essence," Ian confirmed.

"Chief says they are on the way," Jeremiah responded.

Ian hung up and handed the phone back to Kat.

"Good thinking on his part for getting that!" he commented, pointing at the phone.

Kat nodded as well. She gripped the phone and held it to her chest and cast a worried glance at Ian.

"I guess all we can do now is wait." She shrugged her shoulders, the frigid air slowly not affecting her as much.

Ian cast a quick glance thru the freezer window. He turned and gave her an encouraging smile. "It will just be a few minutes now. Marshall will not burn your cafe down, Kat. He won't," he stated with conviction.

She gave a small smile and then sunk down to a sitting position on a stack of pallets. She did not care about the frozen dough pans she was sitting on. Ian watched as Kat slumped her shoulders and let out a deep sigh. He could still see her shivering. He walked over and knelt down in front of her. He placed his fingers lightly under her chin and raised her face until her eyes met his. "Don't give up," he stated simply.

Kat smiled weakly and shook her head. "It's not that, Ian." She rolled glassy eyes away from his gaze and blinked back tears. He felt her chin quiver and slid his hand to gently cup her face. She briefly closed her eyes as if savoring his touch. She then refocused her eyes on him. "I have full faith that Marshall will get what's coming to him in the next few minutes. The police department will do their job, you will do your job, and everything will be fine."

Ian continued to eye her with concern and lightly rubbed his thumb over her cheek. "Then what's the matter?" he asked.

She looked to him again and he saw that she was fiercely holding back her tears. "Talk to me." He whispered tenderly. She lightly closed her eyes and a tear slipped down her cheek. He gently wiped it away.

"I'm sorry." She sniffed in embarrassment. She cleared her throat and shook her head to clear her thoughts. "I guess I'm just nervous about how everything is going to be once all of this is over," she admitted.

Ian gave her a smile. "That's the best part, Kat." He turned her face to look at him. "You can move on with your life, free of Marshall Thompson, free of Biggs, and free of all the police protection surveying your every move. These are good things." He lightly kissed her forehead. "You have a chance to be happy again, away from all of that."

Kat felt another small tear run down her cheek. She couldn't tell Ian that what made her sad the most was the fact that their charade would be over. That their relationship would end. He was the reason she was depressed thinking about life after all that had happened. She had enjoyed her role as his to protect. The thought of not having him around tugged at her heart. She had fallen in love with a man that was only doing his job. No matter the outcome of the days' events, she would end up with a broken heart. Her cafe could be burned to the ground, or her heart could be cast to the ground. She opened her eyes and saw Ian shift his weight to both his knees. He continued holding her face and began to lean towards her. She felt his breath on her lips.

Ian hated that Kat had to go through all that she had with Marshall Thompson. He loved her, and to see her so beat up about... wait... he *loved* her! The realization slapped him in the face. Yes, he felt it at the banquet, but the realization felt new and lit a determination in his gut. They would make it out of this freezer so he could spend time with her, not as her police protection, but actually pursue her and love her. He leaned towards her amazing lips. He couldn't help himself. She looked scared and vulnerable and gorgeous all at the same time. He knew he had kissed her before, but this... this was different. He felt her breath on his lips, but before he could seal her lips with his own, a loud blast sounded thru the cafe. Kat jolted and jumped from her seat. She ran to the window and peeked out. Ian stood close behind her gazing out as well.

∞

The chief signaled his back up to swarm in on the café. Marshall Thompson's bodyguards fell to the ground instantly. Marshall still stood inside, oblivious to his imminent demise. A loud thud and the police officers stormed through all doors leading into the kitchen.

Marshall turned a stunned expression to the chief and his team. A small smile quirked his lips. He slowly dropped to his knees. "Marshall Thompson, you have the right to remain silent..." As Travis read him his Miranda Rights, the chief stepped in front of his line of vision.

"Well played, Chief Winters. Well played," he commented smugly. The chief stepped around him and reached the freezer. He unlocked the hatch lock and opened the door.

Kat and Ian stumbled out, their legs having a hard time adjusting from the freezing cold to the warm kitchen. Kat faltered and Ian caught her and held her next to his side. She gave a deep cough. He knew the cold had affected her more than it did him. He immediately shouted for a blanket. The chief looked him directly in the eyes. "O'Dell," he stated simply and placed his hand on his shoulder. "Good to have you with us." Ian nodded and immediately escorted Kat out the door. As they cleared the building and headed towards the awaiting ambulance, Sara and Jeremiah emerged from Travis' grey pickup parked on the street. Sara ran straight towards Kat as Ian eased her into the back of the ambulance to be evaluated by the EMTs. She gave Kat a strong hug and sat next to her. Travis shook Ian's hand. Kat looked up as Ian turned to walk back towards the building. He never looked back and that was the last she saw him.

∞

"Do you plan to lock yourself away for the rest of your life?" Jeremiah asked as he swung into the kitchen and grabbed a tray of croissants. He rested it on his shoulder as he studied her. "Still no word from Ian?"

Kat shrugged. "It's expected. The case is over, there is no reason for him to come around so often."

"Kat," Jeremiah began, "you know he had feelings for you. I'm sure he is just busy wrapping stuff up."

"I haven't even seen him at Travis'. I don't think he lives there anymore, and Travis won't say one way or the other, because he's been so busy I barely see him too."

"I'm sure both guys will be back to bugging us as soon as they are able. Chin up." He tapped her chin before turning and walking back into the main dining hall.

Kat plunged her whisk into the bowl before her and began whipping eggs. She knew she could throw the eggs into a standing mixer, but the extra effort and frustration she felt needed an outlet, and at the moment, the eggs satisfied. It felt nice to be back in the kitchen. Though it had taken a couple of weeks to clean the gasoline and the smell out of the place, her routine was back up and running.

The truth behind the jump drive had finally been revealed, and though Kat found the facts somewhat unbelievable, she was satisfied with a conclusion to the chaos. Marshall Thompson had grown a conscience. He had wanted out of the business relationship with Biggs, but Biggs was not willing to release him of his duties. So Marshall had created the jump drive as blackmail, threatening to turn it in as evidence of Biggs' business dealings not only with himself but with others in the city. Biggs could not allow Marshall to leave his services because of all he knew, and he certainly did not want the jump drive to be in wrong hands. That is when Marshall noticed it missing. He assumed Kat had stolen it since she had confronted him about his relationship with Biggs, but turns out Kat was in the clear when his secretary stepped forward. She had taken it. And once Marshall was behind bars, she produced the evidence and explained her reasons. Greed. *Everything always seemed to come down to greed*, Kat thought. The amount of money Biggs paid

Marshall for his services was outlandish, and the secretary had benefited from such a healthy pay increase. She did not wish for the money to stop. So she stole the jump drive from Marshall in order to blackmail Biggs on her own if the payments stopped coming in. Marshall had no clue. Kat shook her head. Though she felt a small tinge of sympathy for Marshall, she was also angered by all that had happened over the last couple of months. Her life had been turned upside down for a simple computer gadget. Sighing, she dumped the eggs into the remaining batter and turned the standing mixer on. Now she would let it work its magic as she started on a different project.

She didn't hear the door open as she rummaged in the freezer, the door propped open by a small door stop. Ian smiled, as he eased onto one of the stools at her work table. He heard her gentle hum, and as she exited the freezer and closed the door, her arms laden with rolls of cookie dough, a small scratch at the back door had her smiling. She had yet to notice him as she laid the dough on the counter and grabbed the small bag of cat food by the door. She opened the back door and Chat, Gato, and Kissa awaited her with frantic meows.

"How are my sweet babies today?" she cooed. "I know, it's been quiet around here, hasn't it? That's a good thing." She poured an oversized helping on the back stoop, watching the cats tumble over one another as they ate. Grinning, she shut the door, washed her hands, and then retrieved her dough. Turning, she froze as her gaze finally landed upon Ian.

"Ian."

He smiled. "Hi Kat."

She walked towards the work table and laid the dough upon the surface, and retrieved one of her knives to slice the dough. As she began her task, he watched as she sliced and placed the frozen dough upon cookie sheets.

"Are you going to look at me?" he asked.

She paused and glanced up, her eyes guarded. "I apologize, but I am having a busy day."

"I can see that." He pointed towards the main dining hall. "Not a bad first day back, hmm?"

"I'm thankful." She nudged the first two trays into the oven and began work on several other rolls of dough.

"I came by to give you some news," Ian continued, noting she avoided eye contact at all costs.

"And what's that?" she asked, as she turned her back to him and began gathering supplies for another mixture he could not identify.

"We caught Biggs."

He knew his words would capture her attention, and as her back stiffened and she turned in shock, he knew he had hit his mark.

"Biggs?"

"Yep." He smiled. "Two days ago."

"What? Where? How?" The questions tumbled out of her as he laughed.

"A very anticlimactic take down, but he is now behind bars, along with Marshall."

She lowered her head and wound her hands in front of her. "Hard to believe it's over."

"It's what we wanted, isn't it?" Ian asked as he rounded the table and reached for her hands. Nervously, she allowed him to lace his fingers with hers. "I've missed you, Kat."

He noticed her jaw tighten and she tilted that pointed chin in the air, a defiance in her eyes. "Oh really? Is that why you have ignored me the last two weeks?"

"I wasn't ignoring you, Kat. I was trying to wrap up the Thompson case and about the time that was happening, we received the lead on Biggs, and I was cast head first into that investigation. I've been trying to take down all the threats against

Katharine E. Hamilton

you so you won't have to look over your shoulder." He slid his hands up to her shoulders until she looked up at him. "Now that the threats are gone, I was hoping I could convince you of one more thing."

"And what is that?" Her voice was sharp as she tried to turn away. He held her in place and she feigned annoyance. Before she could think of another response, his lips closed over hers and she felt what little resolve she possessed melt away. He eased away and pressed his forehead against hers. "I've wanted to do that for the last two months." He grinned as she sniffled back a tear and rolled her eyes. Laughing, he pulled her into a hug. "Maybe we could start over? A real relationship this time. No acting, no pretending. Just you and me. What do you say, Kat? "

Kat stood silent a moment and Ian felt her emotionally pulling away. "Please Kat," he continued, "I love you."

Kat's insides jumped at the words, but before she would confess her own feelings a sly smirk played over her face. "I'm sorry, Detective O'Dell," her voice formal, "but I cannot commit to you unless you accept one condition."

He sighed as if she were killing his patience in a slow and agonizing death. "And what would that be, Kat?"

She nodded towards the meows on the back stoop. "I'm a package deal."

Slowly, he allowed himself to relax and then laughed as he wrapped her into his arms. "I think I can handle that, Ms. Riesling." On a firm kiss, they sealed their future, and the promise of safety, security, and love filled Kat's heart to overflowing, as she stared up at Ian and whispered, "I love you too."

All titles by Katharine E. Hamilton
Available on Amazon and Amazon Kindle

Adult Fiction:
The Unfading Lands
https://www.amazon.com/dp/B00VKWKPES

Darkness Divided, Part Two in
The Unfading Lands Series
https://www.amazon.com/dp/B015QFTAXG

Redemption Rising, Part Three in
The Unfading Lands Series
https://www.amazon.com/dp/B01G5NYSEO

Children's Literature:
The Adventurous Life of Laura Bell
Susie At Your Service
Sissy and Kat

Short Stories:
If the Shoe Fits

Find out more about Katharine and her works at:
www.katharinehamilton.com

Social Media is a great way to connect with Katharine. Check her out on the following:

Facebook: Katharine E. Hamilton
https://www.facebook.com/Katharine-E-Hamilton-282475125097433/

Twitter: @AuthorKatharine
Instagram: AuthorKatharine

Contact Katharine:
khamiltonauthor@gmail.com

ABOUT THE AUTHOR

Katharine E. Hamilton started her writing career a decade ago by creating fun-filled stories that have taken children on imaginative adventures all around the world. By using her talents of imagery and suspense to illustrate the deep, underlying issue of good and evil within us all, Katharine extends the invitation for adventure to adults everywhere. She finds herself drawn time and again by the people behind her adventures and wishes to bring them to life in her stories.

She was born and raised in the state of Texas, where she currently resides on a ranch in the heart of brush country with her husband, Brad, and their son, Everett, and their two furry friends, Tulip and Cash. She is a graduate of Texas A&M University, where she received a Bachelor's degree in History. She finds most of her stories share the love of the past combined with a twist of imagination.

She is thankful to her readers for allowing her the privilege to turn her dreams into a new adventure for us all.

Made in the USA
Columbia, SC
04 October 2017